"Whoever you are—or whatever you are—you're severely hindering my efforts to rid the world of one its most deviant miscreants." The old woman lurched out of the forest, this time without her pail and sack. She slashed the air with her two knives, preparing herself. "I suggest you step out where I can see you. That's my prize in the castle, and I'll be damned if some, some, I don't know, werewolf is going to claim him."

"Werewolf?" Deep laughter came from the other side of the forest, and what the old lady had first mistaken for twisted tree branches—long, jagged animal horns—rose from a bramble patch, followed by the eight-foot-tall hairy beast from which they jutted.

"Do you see a full moon? I don't," the thing said. "And since when do werewolves run around on hooves?" The creature, holding its chain and club, lifted one of its hooves to show the woman.

"Ah, I've indeed heard of you," the woman said. "At least I think you're Saint Nicholas's errand boy."

"Nice to meet you, Frau Perchta." The beast exaggeratedly bowed. "The master knows this is your territory and your time of year."

The thing dropped its chain, but not its club, to let its massive barrel slip off its back. It used one hoof to push the barrel off the road while simultaneously stooping to retrieve the long chain. The hag and the beast assessed each other as they began circling clockwise, twenty feet separating them.

TWELFTH KRAMPUS NIGHT

By Matt Manochio

Dedication

This book is dedicated to my son, Nathan, who has yet to warrant a Krampus visit. Let me stress: *yet*.

Chapter One

Tears streaked down Gisela Walborg's cheeks as she stumbled up the dirt road leading to Vettelberg Castle, named after the Bavarian mountain on which it stood.

Uncommon for peasants, Gisela wrapped a thick fox-fur cloak around her white double-apron dress to shield herself from the winter chill. She tucked her long flaxen hair under a circular white wimple—making her look more like a nun than a distraught seamstress.

The rest of the villagers living at the mountain's foot theorized—sometimes sordidly—how her family could afford a fur worn by upper society.

Stole it off a dead noble.

Whored herself to a lord.

But the villagers accepted the comely seventeen-year-old girl's good fortune while envying it all the same.

Gisela couldn't control her crying and slouched against a tall fir tree, resting her head against her forearm to protect it from the cold bark.

"I can't live this way," she mewled between sputtered breaths. "How can I possibly explain it without crushing everyone I love?" She pounded the tree and continued bawling.

"Don't tell anyone!" came a voice too cheerful for the occasion. "If nobody needs to know, then why bother saying anything at all?"

Gisela turned to see a smiling old woman standing in the road.

"People spend entire lives with bottled-up secrets and live quite happily. The sooner you realize that and cease feeling sorry for yourself, the happier you'll be."

Gisela knew not what to make of the unwelcome interference. The old woman's face—from its long hook nose to pointy chin—creased with leathery wrinkles as she smiled. She carried in her left hand a simple wooden bucket, and had slung over her back a large sack—full of what, Gisela couldn't say, but the old woman carried it with ease.

"I'm not the type to keep things pent up inside of me," Gisela said. "And this is something I will not be able to hide forever."

"Tell me then, my dear. It will make you feel better."

"I don't know you."

"Nor I you, but you are clearly distressed and, honestly, a mark for marauders who prowl these woods." The old woman stepped closer to comfort Gisela, who saw a gummy grin with teeth she could count on one hand.

"I can get to the castle on my own—thank you for your worry." Gisela straightened herself and tried marching past the woman, who, despite her small stature and hunched back, darted to block her path.

"You're in no condition to walk by yourself," she said. "Allow me to join you at least part of the way until I'm sure you're close enough to the castle where thieves dare not tread."

Gisela controlled her breathing and assessed the woman—still smiling, her hazel eyes twinkling with anticipation.

"Your bucket's empty," Gisela said. "Are you out for water? And do you need help carrying your sack?"

"Perceptive, my dear. I live not far from here and could use a diversion before heading to the stream. And my sack is light, thank you all the same. Now, your predicament. Let me guess—man troubles?"

"That's really none of your concern."

The old woman nodded. "*Man troubles.* I thought so. Tell me his name, what did he do to you?"

She looked harmless enough to Gisela, who took a few steps up the fir-tree-lined path to the castle, waiting for the woman to catch up. Gisela puzzled over the lady's leather boots—or more precisely, what they covered. The right boot appeared normal—dirty and worn, but normal. The other looked flattened and stretched, as if a duck paddle filled it. But the old woman's fluid movement indicated it posed no impediment.

"Thank you, my dear. Hearing the problems of the young takes me back many decades. You think you have problems now? Just wait. So, how did he harm you?"

"It's not what he did to me—it's what I did to *him*." Gisela soldiered on, slowing down to allow the old woman, wearing a thick black fur cloak over a gray cloth dress, to keep pace.

"Oh, dear, you hurt him? I'm sorry. That's never easy." The woman tucked a grimy length of dislodged black hair underneath a red headscarf as they walked. "Did you spurn his advances and he not handle it well?"

"If only." Gisela felt oddly at ease around the woman, who seemed concerned with her plight. The lady's cheerful voice wrapped around Gisela, soothing her forward both in steps and conversation. "He's one of the most handsome men in these parts, and I never thought he'd take the slightest interest in me. But I had a chance encounter with him. I sew, mend garments— it's what I'm good at. It's how I help my family eat. So it was just me and him. I was sizing up his chest to prepare a new outfit that his family ordered for him."

"Is this man young like you?"

"A year's difference, if that. I placed my hands on his chest, felt how strong he was under his shirt and looked at him, stared at him—and he at me. I ran my hands up and down his arms— his muscles bulged. I couldn't contain myself. Our lips moved toward one another's at the same moment. We kissed. Long and deeply."

The old woman's eyes widened, enjoying the story. "I would imagine. I mean, *look* at you. Such beauty."

The two women ambled along the inclined road, seeing the castle's towers and gray stone walls rising over the treetops— but the massive structure still stood a distance away, and the old lady slowed to catch her breath.

"I've kissed a few men in my day—not recently, as I'm sure you've surmised." The old woman cackled to herself, a shrill, echoing laugh that spooked nearby birds.

Gisela nervously chuckled. "We didn't just kiss." She paused and waited for her companion's laughter to die.

The woman stiffened. "I see. This is serious business then. What is this young man's name?"

"To tell you would start spreading word of my own death. It would bring shame to my family. It can never get out—at least not now." Gisela halted the old woman, who had begun to wheeze the higher they climbed. "We ravaged each other in the fitting room. We were like animals. Feral beasts tearing off each other's clothing, licking each other's flesh. Tasting each other's juices. I can't believe I'm telling you this!"

Gisela blushed, and her good-hearted laugh was the first time she had expressed anything close to happiness before the old woman.

"I told you talking would make you feel better," she needled the girl. "So what happened for you to have hurt him so?"

"I took all of him inside me."

The old woman shot Gisela a queer glance. "I doubt he felt hurt by that."

"No. But it was more than a month ago—and now I carry his child."

An animal growled, a perverse drumroll, deep from within the forest. Both Gisela and the woman looked to their left off the path, seeing nothing but bare-limbed trees interspersed with spruces.

"He knows, and the only other person I've told is my best friend," Gisela nervously continued, looking in the direction of the grumbling. "And I cannot bring myself to tell her everything, like the father's name—even though I swore her to secrecy and trust her. It's that terrible. So many lives would be ruined."

A big, brown animal zoomed across a distant glade, still within the women's view, followed by more growls.

"We should go." The old woman swung the sack and held it in the same hand as the bucket and then seized Gisela's forearm—the grip's strength surprised the girl—and led her off the path, away from the growl and into the woods.

"Where are you taking me?"

"My hovel is not far from here. We *must* take shelter."

Gisela tried wrenching her arm free, but the old lady's grasp wouldn't give. They bounded over dead leaves, wove around trees, and soon realized the grumbling had stopped. The women kept their guard up, though, upon seeing, one hundred feet deeper into the woods, a brown hairy mass running through the trees, obscured by brush and branches, until it took refuge behind one.

"I must get to the castle." Gisela pulled the old woman back toward the path. "I'll run if I have to. I have a knife if I encounter an animal." She pointed to her belt, displaying a small hunting blade she'd swiped when her father wasn't looking.

"My dear, you have no idea what is out there."

"What does that mean? Let me go."

The old woman released Gisela, who stumbled backward toward the road.

"If you continue onward, you could be attacked, or worse. I want nothing to happen to you on that path."

Gisela saw they were far enough from the road so no passersby would likely see them. Whatever the animal was, it hadn't moved from its spot behind the tree. *Perhaps it skulked away*, Gisela thought. She tugged the fox cloak around her, more out of nerves than to gain warmth.

The animal's grumbling—the kind the women had first heard when walking the path—resumed and grew louder, closer, as if the beast making it had followed them.

Gisela looked around, disoriented, uncertain of the way. She looked at the old woman and expected to see fright in her eyes, but instead saw annoyance.

"Whatever animal is out there, I'm sure we're not in danger," Gisela said. "They usually run away at the sight of humans. Let's circle around to the path. It can't be far."

The old woman stood a good foot shorter than Gisela and balefully looked at her. "Don't you know what day it is?"

Gisela hadn't expected the question. "Tuesday?"

"*No.* I mean, the significance of *this* very date—January fifth." The old woman waited for Gisela to answer but got a vacant stare instead. "Don't you know what could happen to you on this day, the peril you could be in? Your parents must keep you sheltered."

Gisela jogged her memory. "Yes, it's Twelfth Night, the night of the Epiphany. But it's the last thing on my mind."

A bear cub scampered from behind a tree and appeared startled upon seeing two women, who instantly took notice of the little bruin.

Gisela exhaled, relieved. "The animal we saw back there. Nothing but a baby."

The old woman turned pensive, then worried. "The growling—it must be the cub's—" she said before a full-throated roar interrupted her, shocking both her and Gisela's attention away from the baby. They turned to see what they guessed to be the bear's mother charging them.

Gisela fumbled for the small knife in her belt. The old woman pushed Gisela behind her, dropped her bucket and sack and glowered at the bear. She flapped her cloak behind her and spread her arms wide, as if opening them to embrace the mother, straightened herself and shrieked.

The old woman's howl frightened the mother bear enough so that it ceased running and began skidding on its paws over the leaves, trying to stop itself, clearly not wanting anything to do with the little old lady.

Gisela peeked behind to see the frightened cub running into the deep woods.

The old woman drew breath and roared again. Gisela swore the woman's voice pulsated from her mouth, *pushing* the bear to flee in the opposite direction.

The woods quieted. The old woman looked at the forest floor and grabbed her bucket.

"As I said, I didn't want anything happening to you on the path."

"Thank you," Gisela said. "Nor I you."

"Now, while I didn't want to do this *here*, I suppose here is as good a place as any. We seem to be far enough away."

"Far away enough from whom?"

The woman placed the bucket before Gisela's feet. "Could you please stand still, my dear?"

Gisela glanced at the bucket and up to the woman. "I can, but I don't underst—"

The old woman reached both hands behind her back and then swiped her arms forward and across Gisela's belly.

Gisela barely registered the unsheathing and slitting sounds. She looked down to her belly to see a waterfall of intestines splattering into the bucket.

Gisela didn't scream despite the pain. She gasped, shock overtaking her body.

The old woman licked blood off both sides of her blades, stowing one behind her back and keeping the other handy. She reached into the yawning gash and yanked the remaining guts into the bucket, cutting free the small intestine after she deemed enough had coiled in the pail. She pushed Gisela—still alive but with her life draining fast—to land on her back, and knelt over the gushing wound.

The old woman sheathed the knife and retrieved the sack. She pulled out what Gisela could not identify by sight but by smell—straw. The old woman stuffed every strand from the sack into Gisela's belly, which appeared to have exploded, the skin flaps resembling blossomed flower petals.

The last thing Gisela saw before closing her eyes was the old woman's shaky right hand trying to thread twine through the eye of a large sewing needle.

She felt the old woman bring her stomach flaps together, followed by inexplicable pinpricks.

"Harlot." The old woman spit on the girl, who died thinking she'd delivered a baby in a way unintended by God.

Chapter Two

Beate Klothilda's family had little money and, like the rest of the villagers, had to do whatever they could to scratch out a living. And for women that meant sewing. Beate didn't care that her wedding dress would appear to be made of rags—it essentially was—and that despite her best intentions to bathe herself, the nobles would always consider her dirty if they ever deigned to leave the castle and enter the village.

None of that mattered to Beate. She would marry in a week's time her childhood sweetheart, Heinrich Kluber, around whom she wrapped her arms, lovingly embracing him as they rode his family's lone horse, Uli, from the castle to the village.

Heinrich, assistant to his village blacksmith father, had delivered to the castle's burgmann newly hammered knives and pike heads, for the castle blacksmith no longer had the ability to forge anything—dysentery having claimed him a week earlier.

"I can't say it's good fortune for our family to prosper while another man's starves, but with all the work we've been getting, you might just have a fancy wedding after all." Heinrich held steady Uli's reins, imagining the horse was thankful that both saddlebags were now empty of their iron loads.

"I'm just glad you're back, love." Beate ran her hands up and down her beau's chest and stomach. "Any number of things could've happened while you were away."

"It was worth the two weeks I was gone—one of the most successful trade trips my family has ever had to France. Besides, I didn't need to make anything. My father took care of that. All I needed to do was be the salesman. I'm pretty good at it."

"Think there's a chance your father will work in the castle?"

Beate said. "He'd be under the protection of the baron."

"My father's too old to fight, and it would be expected of him. Me, on the other hand..." Heinrich let it linger.

"You'd fight?"

"I would. I'd just make certain there were hundreds of knights standing in front of me." Heinrich wore a long-sleeved white linen shirt, covered by a brown waistcoat. Deerskin breeches and leather boots completed the ensemble. Nobody would mistake how he earned his living.

"You could be killed." She caressed the top of his head, her fingers running over his short black hair.

"The baron is on good terms with the surrounding nobles. It's been unexpectedly nonviolent in recent years."

"That won't last." Beate hugged Heinrich, not just because she loved him, but because of his body heat. Although her woolen dress was scratchy, her linen undergarments kept the discomfort to a minimum. Her sheepskin cloak added an extra layer of warmth. "I'd rather you be in the village to protect us and our families."

Heinrich slowed Uli and looked over his shoulder to address his fiancée.

"We're merely conjecturing, love. The baron seems comfortable with the arrangement in place. My father can travel to the castle and I can work in the village, or vice versa. Having two blacksmiths is a luxury. I plan on being in the village with you for a long time." He steadied himself and turned some more and ran his fingers down Beate's shoulder-length brown hair and kissed her. "Fear not."

He prodded Uli to trot the trail.

"How's the dress coming along?"

"Gisela's almost done with it." Beate smiled, thinking of her best friend. "Since we were children she'd talk about making *my* wedding dress."

"What if you wanted to make your own? You're as good a seamstress as Gisela."

"I'm *not*. But thank you. It's one less thing I've had to worry about, and it allows me to earn a living rather than fretting about my own project. Gisela's doing it for free—she insists."

"That *is* kind of her."

They ambled down the path a few minutes without speaking, listening to the whistling wind, occasionally shielding their eyes from it, before Beate spoke.

"No reservations? About our wedding?"

"I think we were destined to marry when we learned we were both born on the same day," Heinrich said. "I'm surprised we didn't marry sooner. My parents did when they were seventeen."

"We'll be eighteen in a week. There won't be much of a difference. And I think it's appropriate that we marry *on* our birthday. I'm glad you suggested it, love." Beate thought for a moment. "Love—that's one advantage peasants have over the nobles, for the most part. We marry for love, they marry for land. A marriage isn't healthy if you have plenty of space but don't truly appreciate the person you're sharing it with."

"It's a good thing our parents arranged our marriage and that we just so *happen* to love each other—some aren't as fortunate," Heinrich said.

"Well, hello, young lovebirds!"

Heinrich yanked Uli to stop him from hitting an old woman standing in the road.

"Watch where you're going!" Heinrich said.

"Why don't you watch where *you're* going? I was standing here all the while you were chatting with your beloved betrothed." The old woman expressed no animosity.

"I'm sorry, I didn't see you," he said.

Beate, still clutching Heinrich, poked out her head to see who stood in their way.

"You could hear us?" she said.

"Not so much *you*," the old woman said. "The young man's voice carries, and I'm glad it does. Hearing about young love makes me tingly. And truly good women like you deserve nothing but a man who'll cherish and respect them. Here."

The old woman walked to Uli's side, both riders eyeing her suspiciously. "Open your hand, dear, I mean you no harm."

Beate cautiously extended her open left hand, ready to yank it back, but there was no need. The old woman clutched Beate's hand with both of hers, and when she released it, Beate held a silver coin the size of her palm.

"Better in the hand than in the shoe, right?" the old woman said, smiling.

"What?" It was Heinrich.

Beate was too distracted to reply. She'd seen silver coins from a distance when the wealthy bought the most expensive clothes during her visits to the castle. But now to hold one?

"Thank you," she squeaked.

"No thanks necessary, my dear." The old woman walked toward the castle. She called over her shoulder, "It's a solidus, my dear—all for you. Try not to cry on your wedding day."

Heinrich looked at Beate and then to the coin, whose face depicted a bust of Jesus Christ—His hand raised in benediction, a cross behind Him—and lettering they did not recognize. The obverse portrayed a man—they knew not who—standing on steps, holding a cross potent.

The couple looked behind them and saw no trace of the old woman.

"Beate, *hide it*. Put it away. Who knows who's watching?" Heinrich said through gritted teeth.

As casually as she could, Beate slipped the coin into a small pocket she had sewn on the inside of her cloak. "Go, love," she whispered, and kissed his cheek.

They rode Uli in silence while keeping vigilant of their surroundings. Heinrich hesitated farther up the path, and then slowed Uli when he spotted a woman sitting against a tall evergreen, her legs sticking into the road.

"Someone's napping, B." Heinrich pointed fifty feet ahead to his right. "At least I hope someone's napping."

"Bandits? It could be a trap." Beate had heard the stories of criminals springing from the woods, slitting innocent throats and absconding with whatever they could fleece from the bodies.

Heinrich patted the baselard sheathed on his belt and surveyed the landscape, seeing nothing unusual. "I'll just keep going."

He prodded Uli almost to run but reined him in upon

hearing Beate. "Gisela, no!"

Beate didn't wait for Uli to stop moving but slid off the horse, rushing to her friend.

Heinrich couldn't see the woman's face, as her head drooped toward her belly. "How do you know it's her?"

"I'd recognize the fox fur anywhere." Beate was shocked the cloak hadn't been pilfered. She kneeled before her friend, unable to comprehend the bloody mass that was her bloodstained belly, oozing crimson into her shredded white dress.

She placed the back of her hand to Gisela's cheek and shivered at its iciness. Beate used both hands to gently lift Gisela's head and cried while looking at lifeless blue eyes.

Heinrich hopped off Uli, holding the horse's reins in one hand and unsheathing his dagger with the other. "We can't do anything for her here. We have to warn the rest of the village."

"Oh no, that means her bab—" Beate stopped herself midsentence, remembering the promise she had made to Gisela never to divulge her now-dead secret.

"That means what?" Heinrich stooped down, trying to make eye contact. "I don't understand."

"It's nothing, love. I don't know what I'm saying, but I can't leave her." Beate lowered Gisela's head, glanced to her friend's belly and recoiled. "Someone stitched her up!"

Heinrich squinted and blanched at the running stitches that formed a gruesome and misshapen X on Gisela's belly. Bloodstained straw poked from the occasional seam. Beate fingered a stalk tip near her friend's navel.

"What was she doing out here?" Beate stood and hugged Heinrich, sobbing into his shoulder.

"She was supposed to fit me for clothing in a few hours, after our deer hunt," said a man behind them.

Beate and Heinrich whirled to see Lord Wilhelm, the baron's son, looking at Gisela and not them.

So shocked were Beate and Heinrich, they forewent bows and curtsies.

"We found her like this. She's my fiancée's closest friend," Heinrich said. "Surely you don't think we did this."

Wilhelm, sitting atop a black courser, eyed the body.

"So much for my new tunic being ready on time. And my brother's," he said as an afterthought and looked at the shaken pair. "And no, I don't think you killed her. I would wager your dagger and clothes would be drenched if you had."

"Boy, sheath your sword," commanded one of the two knights on horseback accompanying Wilhelm. They all were dressed similarly in chain-mail tunics covering woolen gambesons. Wilhelm, who wore a black bear-fur cloak, kept a longbow and a full quiver behind his back. The knight who had spoken aimed a crossbow at Heinrich's chest.

Heinrich did as ordered by the hulking knight, who in kind lowered his crossbow. Wilhelm brought back his cloak's hood, revealing curly brown hair and brown eyes. Beate spotted his dimpled chin. *It figures*, she thought. Both of the baron's sons—Wilhelm born a year before Beate and Heinrich; Karl, the younger, a year later—made the ladies swoon. Whether Karl was as arrogant as Wilhelm, Beate could only guess. She guessed yes.

"We should get you back to the castle," the knight said. "Let these two worry about informing the village."

"Patience, Otto," Wilhelm replied. "You there, girl, look at me."

Frightened, but not enough *not* to feel insulted, she did. "Yes, my lord. My name is Beate."

"You've accompanied at times this poor girl to the castle to help fit the nobles, correct? I've seen you there. Normally I forget what peasants look like, but you and your friend are notable exceptions."

Beate controlled her breathing and tempered her rage. "I have, my lord, on occasions when the baron's seamstresses were either unavailable or dead."

"Well, then you shall accompany our party back to the castle to fit me and my brother."

"But my friend!" she shouted, not in anger but disbelief.

"Be careful the way you address Lord Wilhelm," called the second knight in a tsk-tsk tone.

"Easy, Hans. You too, Otto." Wilhelm held up his hand to keep his guards at bay and continued with the peasants. "You have my sympathies, but my tunic takes precedence. You see, the baron wants my outfit ready for my brother's wedding. Not only that, Karl has returned from a two-month trip to Spain, and I believe your unfortunate friend there did only cursory measurements on him. Much work needs doing on his. So you'll need to fit him posthaste. Big event, you see. Then again, *all* of our events are big."

The knights laughed, as if on cue.

"My lord, I respectfully ask you allow me to take my friend, Gisela—she has a name—back to her family. The entire village must know about this. To protect themselves."

Heinrich stayed quiet, eyeing Wilhelm, trying not to show his contempt. "With all respect, my lord, will Beate be paid for her services?"

Beate looked at him, agog. "Heinrich!"

"But of course your fine maiden will be paid—handsomely, I might add, as you've already been inconvenienced, and that is not lost on me," Wilhelm said. "I would imagine your friend's sewing kit is on her body somewhere, and I would suggest you find it. The regular seamstress is unable to perform her duties."

A small gasp escaped Beate and she covered her lips with her fingertips. "I beg your pardon for asking, but is she sick? Fighting plague? Smallpox? Typhoid?"

Wilhelm feigned surprise. "Goodness no! Nothing that would directly endanger the castle's denizens. Bandits merely raped and killed her. Dagger to the heart. Relatively painless. The same cannot be said of the fate met by her attackers. It's fortunate the baron and his hunting party caught them in the act. Happened not far from here, actually. Their capture allowed us to test the new breaking wheel. I'm pleased to say it works. Splendidly."

Beate knew not what a breaking wheel was and never wanted to find out. "The seamstress's name, my lord, what was it?"

"Who knows? But you'll have at your disposal her sewing kit that I'm certain contains instruments that your little ones do not. Now, I suggest we move along. I will send Hans here to warn the village and to return your friend to her family. Your blacksmith friend here—" Wilhelm looked Heinrich up and down, "—may escort you."

Heinrich leaned in to Beate's ear before she could respond. "I know you're hurting, and Gisela's family *will* know about her, just as Lord Wilhelm just said."

"I can't leave." Her voice cracked.

"I'm thinking about us too. This could be a chance for you to escape the village for something better. That's what I'm hoping to do with my smithing. This is an opportunity for *us*, for our lives together after we marry."

"Learn how to whisper, Heinrich," Wilhelm said. "But your man is correct. Good help is indeed hard to find, and, sadly, easily wasted." He looked at Gisela. "So pretty too."

Beate wiped away her tears and glowered at Heinrich—he had a good point, but it came at a most inappropriate moment, and *why* he couldn't see that, she'd never know.

"It's the Walborg family," she called to Hans. "Ask for them. The villagers will know where to send you." Beate kneeled for a final time next to her friend, feeling around Gisela's dress and eventually finding a small leather satchel, loose and worn. Beate knew immediately what it held.

"I'll make sure your mother gets your kit back." She kissed Gisela's forehead and wept as Heinrich mounted Uli and pulled Beate up to sit behind him.

"Place the girl over Hans's horse. Secure her somehow," Wilhelm said to Otto, an older knight near forty who kept his gray hair cut short, but his beard full to cover skin pockmarked by smallpox scars.

Wilhelm reached into a small saddlebag and pulled out two gold coins, flipping one to Hans.

"Return her to the village with the baron's condolences, and give them the noble." He turned to Beate and Heinrich and tossed the second coin their way. Heinrich caught it and was immediately told by Wilhelm, "Give it to your lady. It's advance payment for her emergency services." And then, speaking to them like children: "It's a golden coin from England—my father obtained a bunch of them. Don't ask me how."

The knights did as told. Otto awkwardly draped Gisela—her

body forming a human horseshoe—on Hans's horse's rear, securing it with rope the big knight carried for such situations. Hans bounded away, one hand holding the reins, the other pressing down the body to keep it from falling.

Wilhelm smiled at the disbelieving couple. "Now, Beate and Heinrich, let's get on with our day. I'd like to return to the castle while there's still light outside."

Heinrich handed the coin to Beate, who hid it without having to be told. They followed Wilhelm, with Otto bringing up the rear. The castle soon towered over them, and they waited for flunkies to lower the drawbridge and raise the portcullis.

The massive spiked gate began its ascent and revealed a younger version of Wilhelm sitting atop a white horse.

"Karl, so good to see you," Wilhelm said. "I've brought a seamstress who will fit both you and me for your wedding."

Karl prodded his horse to amble to Wilhelm's party. The baron's youngest son, shorter and stockier than Wilhelm, had his brother's brown eyes and hair, although Karl's was receding, a sure sign he'd be bald in five years.

"This isn't the one I remember from the last time—Gisela, I believe."

"Yes, a pity. Gisela was murdered earlier this day—bandits most likely." Wilhelm made it sound like a mild inconvenience as he described Gisela's condition when they'd left her with Hans.

"Her friend here—" Wilhelm nodded and flashed his eyes at her, for he'd clearly forgotten her name.

"Beate." She forced a smile.

"Yes, Beate here is a seamstress who will take her place for now. And this is her lucky fiancé, Heinrich, who's been gracious enough to bring her to the castle."

Karl, dressed like his brother in layers of linen, wool and chain-mail, with a brown fur cloak shrouding most of his body, looked them both over and spoke to Beate. "I am sorry to hear about your friend. She seemed like a very capable seamstress, and a better person."

"That's kind of you to say, my lord." Beate detected sincerity in Karl's voice that was nonexistent in anything that Wilhelm had previously said to her.

"And Heinrich, it's good of you to bring her here." Karl noticed the way Heinrich caressed her hands that met around his waist as she hugged him. "And clearly you care for her. I wish I could say the same about *my* future wife."

"Let's not get into that here, Karl. You'll learn to enjoy your wife's company as I have mine. And if she ever gets mad at you, simply provide her jewelry. That works for me. I think she picked a fight with me last week just to get a new bracelet."

"Arranged marriages are nonsense," Karl muttered to himself, then looked at the peasants. "And you're right, no sense bothering Beate and Heinrich with my woes. But I am happy for you, really. Please, as long as you're here providing this service, I insist you have a nice meal. We can stable your horse and feed him too."

Heinrich and Beate stared at each other, not knowing how to accept such unforeseen generosity.

"My little brother, what a softie." Wilhelm looked to Beate. "He takes after our mother. I don't believe our father has spoken to a peasant in a year, and that was merely an apology from over his shoulder after accidentally running one down with his horse. Always look both ways before you cross the road, you know."

Mumfred, the steward who oversaw the castle's daily operations, wandered over to the gathering and was joined by two squires. Quick introductions and explanations were made.

"Have the kitchen prepare them anything they like," Karl said. "The cooks are looking for something to bake, seeing that my parents aren't here."

Mumfred, a tall bald man whose eyes were spaced a little too far apart for Beate's comfort, assessed the peasants. "Very well, my lord. I suppose anything will be a nice departure from moldy bread."

"That's not necessary, *Mummy*." Karl knew Mumfred despised the nickname. "They are my guests—our guests." He looked at Wilhelm, who rolled his eyes. "And they shall be treated as such. And I prefer you feed them now so I can get in some hunting before it gets dark." Karl tilted back his head so everyone would notice the longbow over his shoulder.

"We just came back from one," Wilhelm said. "We didn't see a single deer out there."

Two knights rode their horses behind Karl and stopped. "Ready, my lord," one said.

"Then you weren't looking hard enough," Karl said to his brother, and then to the knights, "Victor, Mathias, let's go!" Karl charged off, calling to Beate and Heinrich, "Enjoy your meal. See you soon."

"I suppose a little more time outdoors couldn't hurt—you up for it, Otto?" said Wilhelm.

"Yes, my lord."

Just as Wilhelm prepared to depart, a fierce, prolonged roar bolted through the air from behind, whooshing by them and through the portcullis's opening

"Well, at least we know there's *one* big animal out there," Wilhelm said to Otto. "Let's go find it!"

None of them knew it, but the roaring thing was the reason Gisela—but not Hans—reached the village.

Chapter Three

Hans removed his hand from Gisela's bouncing corpse—confident Otto had tied the body around the horse's frame enough so that it wouldn't slide off. He didn't especially enjoy the prospect of mingling with peasants, but felt compassion, knowing he'd soon devastate a family without touching his sword.

The girl was *pretty,* he thought. *There's no way she didn't suffer.*

Hans had seen his share of cruelty doled out to enemies of the lord to whom he'd pledged himself. He'd heard about ordinances dictating that anyone caught stripping bark off a tree would have his belly slit. A length of intestine was yanked out and nailed to the trunk, and then the unfortunate soul was made to circle the tree so long as any part of his gut was left in his body.

A twisted dance around the maypole, Hans thought. *And that was just for stripping bark. What's the big deal about stripping bark? Just chop off my head and be done with it.*

Soon the road would cease its decline and open toward a cobblestone-lined village a distance from the mountain's base. He estimated it to be three o'clock, time enough to dispose of the body and return to the castle before nightfall. Danger grew whenever one lost sight of the castle.

Instinct prodded him to unsling his crossbow from his back and stop his horse in the middle of the road. He heard and saw no movement, but he knew someone was watching.

"I am one of the baron's knights." He kept the crossbow at a downward angle, ready to raise and aim it. "My lord knows my whereabouts and will be expecting my return. My disappearance will mean my fellow knights *will* come looking for me, and if you are from the village and they learn this, it will not bode well for you or your family."

Hans waited for a reply. Just silence, the kind that stoked uneasiness.

"I seek nothing more than to return this murdered girl to her family. Walborg's the name. I shall reward you should you assist in me in finding the parents."

"Leave the girl."

Hans aimed the bow to where the deep voice originated. He saw nothing but clustered fir trees, enough to shield a body.

"Unless you are a relative and can prove it, I will not." Hans pivoted back and forth, listening for movement. "Show yourself."

"I only want the girl. She means nothing to you. Leave her and ride back to your lord." The rough voice seemed angered by having to converse.

"I'm afraid I cannot do that. I have my orders."

"Then I will take the girl and will leave you dead."

Hans knew exactly what false bravado sounded like—this sounded *nothing* like it. Although his face expressed confidence and resolve, he couldn't help but think that whoever addressed him from within the woods would stay true to his word.

"Threatening a knight is punishable by death. And when I identify your relatives in the village, they'll suffer too."

Hans didn't expect amused laughter, or the response that chilled him: "Raze the village for all I care. Kill everyone in it. Give me the girl. Now."

Hans heard a few heavy clinks of a chain, sounds that made his horse fidget. "Easy, Hrolf, easy," he whispered into Hrolf's ear to steady him, and then to the forest, "If you were serious and a competent shot, you'd have arrowed me by now. You're bluffing."

"I don't use bows or arrows. Nor swords. Against you, all I need are my bare hands. And hooves."

"What?" Hans said, then shuddered when the spot in the trees where he'd aimed his bow roared at him. Hrolf reared, sending Hans, still holding his crossbow, tumbling over Gisela's body and landing butt-first on the ground. Hrolf bounded for the village but had gotten not twenty feet when a large chain flew from behind tree trunks and wrapped around the horse's neck. The wielder yanked back the chain, and the sound of the horse's neck snapping echoed through the branches. Hrolf collapsed on his side, pinning Gisela's lower body to the ground.

The wielder dropped the chain. Hans saw an immense figure striding behind the trees, making its way toward the shaken knight.

Hans aimed his bow, timed the thing's movements and fired an arrow the moment the figure strode past an oak tree. The arrow sizzled and hit its target square.

Hans didn't attempt to reload. He dropped the weapon next to him and remained seated, marveling at what appeared from the woods with an arrow's fletchings and nock jutting from a brown, hairy rib cage.

"Ouch," the creature mocked.

Now Hans knew what it meant by hooves, for it stood on two of them, the top of its head hovering eight feet above ground. The two twisted horns atop its skull made it ten feet.

The creature plucked the arrow from its side and almost flicked it away like a used toothpick, but refrained at the last second.

"I know you," Hans said, awestruck by the thing his parents had warned him about when he was a child who had scoffed at the idea of its existence. "But it's January. It's over. And I'm no longer a boy."

The creature stood in front of Hans, resting its clawed hands on its hips, looking at the knight the way a parent might a misbehaving child.

"Correct. You're now an unthinking yes-man. You should've stayed a boy. I never came for you then—you must've done something right. But that was long ago. Today you turn a blind eye to despicable acts perpetrated by those who employ you."

"Take the girl, she's yours." Hans dove back to reality.

"You don't think I'm aware of that? It's what I'm planning on doing to *you* that's keeping me here."

The thing brought the arrow up to its eye level, examining

it, and then looked down to the knight and grinned to reveal all of its fangs. It then held up its pointer finger, making certain Hans could see its curved talon. "I have an idea. Let's you and I go for a walk."

The creature's hand, when placed over Hans's screaming mouth, concealed almost all of the slowly dying knight's head, muffling his anguish. It finished with Hans and loped to the horse and used the same bloodstained fingernail to slice the rope binding Gisela. It lifted the horse by the tail and gingerly picked up Gisela, seeing what he'd expected but needing to be sure.

"And they say *I* am heartless. You were lucky you were with child a month ago." It held Gisela by her shoulder, her body dangling from its grasp like a used handkerchief. "The master frowns upon harming pregnant women."

It looked at Gisela's belly. "I must show you to the master. He needs to see the frau's handiwork. The master is not without heart either. I am certain he shall have me return you to your family."

It reached over its head, still holding Gisela, and lowered her body into a tall and fat barrel it had strapped to its back.

It retrieved the chain from around Hrolf's neck and lowered the links into the barrel next to the girl.

It left the horse to be picked on by a mother bear and her cub, both of which would be scared away by knights who would later find Hans, slouched face-first against a tree, his intestines wound several times around the trunk, the gut's end stuck in place by a crossbow arrow.

Chapter Four

"Do you think he'll come for us?" The girl, Anna, was ten years old, as was her identical twin sister, Sarah. Both girls cowered in the corner of the family's one-room wattle-and-daub house, the cold and their nerves jiggling their blonde pigtails.

"He knows when Mother and Father go to the village—he counts on it," Sarah said. They scrunched themselves into little balls, covering themselves with a big woolen blanket, their knees tucked under their chins. Waning daylight filtered through two small, shuttered windows, which both girls focused on, hoping his shadow wouldn't cut the sunlight.

"It's been a while since he last visited. Maybe he no longer fancies us," Anna whispered. "We've been good girls, not told anyone about him."

"Nobody would believe us anyway. Said he'd kill us. I believe him."

"It's punishment—that's what it feels like to me," Anna said.

"That's not the way he sees it. He *enjoys* it, laughs at our pain."

"But why *us*? Of all the children who live in and around the village, why does he pick us?"

Sunlight flickered through the latched shutters, fast enough so that the girls couldn't tell if a bird or their imaginations caused it.

"How do you know we're the only ones?" Sarah pulled the wool up to the ridge of her nose so that only her blue eyes peeked above the blanket.

The knock on the door caused them to bounce on their bottoms.

"He *never* knocks," Anna said.

Sarah knew it wasn't him either—he always opened the door, unannounced, and snatched them up one by one, leaving the other too terrified to help. Neither moved to answer the knock.

"Anna? Sarah? Are you in there?" came a grandmotherly voice.

"Who do we know who sounds like that?" Anna whispered to Sarah.

"You don't know me at all, but I know *you*," the reply came cheerfully.

The girls stared at each other, each thinking, *How can she hear us?*

"Or were you expecting someone else, my dearies? I think you'll prefer my company over anybody else's. I understand you're both good seamstresses, like your mother. I'd love to see your work."

Anna swept the blanket aside and stood.

"*No*," her sister pleaded.

"Maybe if he sees someone in here with us, he'll skip our house."

Sarah thought about it and enthusiastically nodded yes.

Anna walked to the wooden door, which rested on hinges and had no lock. It took some effort for her to push it open and see standing outside an old woman holding a bucket and sack.

"Which one are you, little one?"

"I'm Anna."

"May I please come in, Anna?"

He could be making his way through the woods now, the girl thought.

"Please do."

The old woman hobbled inside, nudging Anna aside. One lighted candle, centered on a small wooden table, lit the home. Straw had been strewn all over the floor. At night the girls' parents would bring in the family's milking cow so that it wouldn't get stolen, and because its body heat would help warm everyone where they huddled on the floor to sleep. Father slept with a dagger close by because he had built the thatched-roofed house—with the baron's permission—in the woods, away from the village's relative safety.

"That's a wonderful blanket, Sarah." The old woman placed aside her belongings "Bring it here. May I please see it?"

Sarah rose and bunched up the scratchy blanket in her arms and brought it to the woman, who snapped it open to admire it.

"Did you both sew this?" She ran her hands over the blanket, admiring how tightly it'd been stitched.

"We took turns, yes," Sarah said. "It's our first one without Mother's help."

"And what a fine job your mother did teaching you." She handed it back to Sarah and turned to Anna. "It's nearly dinnertime. Where are your parents?"

"Bringing fish back from the village. It won't take long to cook."

"A fine choice to eat on Twelfth Night, would you agree?" the old woman extended her gnarled knuckles to Anna and gently stroked her cheek. "I have something for you."

The old woman reached behind her back to retrieve a silver coin for Anna, who stepped back, not knowing what to expect. "I'll put this on the table for you." She slapped it facedown, a loud clack reverberating off the wood. "And I've not forgotten about you, Sarah." The old woman repeated the process, leaving two silver coins side by side for the girls.

"I'm very pleased with you both, how hard you worked this year on your first blanket. And I'm sure you'll be making more in the year ahead."

"We've already started," Anna said. "Each of us is working on our own."

"That's what I like to hear." The old woman's pleasant demeanor vanished. She looked around the room and shushed the girls when one appeared about to speak.

"Go sit in the corner, the way you were when I first got here. Take the blanket. Now."

Anna and Sarah scampered to the corner and resumed their positions, now terrified because they too felt someone else's presence.

The old woman stooped and blew out the candle, and the girls lost sight of her.

The door was still open, but neither girl had seen her slip out. Sarah gasped when a large figure stood in the doorway.

"Didn't think I was going to arrive, did you?" came a male voice. "How could I pass up such an opportunity? I've been gone so long. I've arranged for your parents to be delayed in the village. They'll be none the wiser. Who would like to be first?"

Neither girl knew which of the baron's sons did unwanted things to them. He never gave his name, only orders to refer to him as "my lord".

"I can never tell you apart, especially in this dark. How your parents do it mystifies me. I suppose parents know their children best. But it's still light enough out so that I can see what I'm doing." He popped open the closed shutters to allow for a little more light. "So, who would like to take off her clothes first?"

The girls knew this was coming. Each wore a dirty cut-down tunic over a simple skirt. Anna began to cry.

The lord slipped off his leather gloves and laid them on the table. "I just want to hold one of you to start. Cuddle a bit. Make you feel nice and warm."

He walked toward the girls, who turned toward each other and hugged, soon sobbing onto each other.

Just as the lord prepared to pounce, the shutters seemed to slam shut at once, followed by the door creaking back toward the house, sealing them into darkness.

The lord and the girls heard a soft cackle coming from the closed door, followed by "I think it goes without saying that you will *not* be getting a silver coin."

He puffed out his chest. "I'm one of the lords of the castle. Leave this instant and speak nothing of this or I shall have you killed."

"Is that so? Well, I'm not setting foot from this house for the foreseeable future, and when I do leave, I have every intention of informing the villagers of what a vile pervert you are. They'll never quite look at the baron the same way."

The lord reached for his knife but realized he'd left it in his horse's saddlebag outside so as not to frighten the girls.

"What? A helpless old woman makes a statement of fact and

your reaction is to grab a blade?"

Without thinking, the lord barreled his way forward, flipping over the table and breaking through the weak door. Wood splintered outward, spooking his horse tied to a tree. He freed his ride and charged through the woods to the main road, looking for his brother.

"Make sure you find your coins, dearies," the old woman called to the quivering girls inside the home. "Now the hunt begins."

The creature, crouching within a bramble patch—the last place the hunters, especially this prim and proper bunch, would dare tread—unfurled its parchment and glanced at a name that hadn't been stricken from the list. One of the men straddled a horse in the middle of the road, waiting for the rest of the hunting party to return. The beast reached behind its back and slowly drew from its barrel a chain, gingerly pulling it so the links would slink over the barrel's lip.

The lord clearly heard it.

That was part of the plan. Let the cretin hear a noise out of place within the woods. While technically not on the list— the creature knew not why—the marked man appeared long overdue for punishment.

Typically the brothers were never far from a knight for protection, but both considered themselves skilled fighters and keen bowmen. The lord circled his horse around the road, scanning the trees and bushes.

"Otto? Mathias? Are you there?"

"Yes, my lord." Otto, followed by Victor and Mathias, galloped to meet him. "Your brother's not far behind us. He was looking for you."

"As I was him. We all seem to get separated so easily. And I see we've not had any luck." The lord saw no kills tied to the knights' horses.

The brothers reunited, and the five men trotted the trail up toward the castle, resigned they'd find nothing that day. Victor held up his hand to halt the procession.

"My lords, up ahead, two bears, eating a—Good *God*, that's Hans's horse."

They lost all interest in hunting and charged the bears, chasing them into the forest. "Damn things should be hibernating." Victor climbed off his horse and caught sight of Hans, gruesomely lashed to a tree by his own entrails.

Without being ordered, Otto dismounted and cut the last gut link tethering Hans to the tree. The intestine trail sickeningly unraveled. Otto roped the dead knight to his horse for the ride home.

"My lords, we must leave here, now," said Otto, who, like Victor, remounted his steed. Mathias had drawn his crossbow and stayed close to the baron's sons, looking for any movement.

"I checked his horse. The saddlebags weren't touched. He still had his weapons," Victor said. "Outright murder. This wasn't a robbery."

Mathias swiveled on his horse and spotted something in the brambles.

"We're being watched, my lords. Move." A thick iron chain exploded from the brambles, smashing Mathias's face, crushing his nose into his skull, penetrating brain, killing him. The chain snapped back into the woods just as Mathias hit the ground.

The brothers drew their longbows and fired a succession of arrows from whence came the chain. Otto, fearless, jumped off his horse and unsheathed his broadsword, waited for the lords to stop firing and immediately hacked into the brambles.

A man screamed from behind them. Otto and the lords turned and gasped when they saw Victor's stomach gushing blood onto his panicked horse's saddle. An old woman in black straddled the horse from behind Victor, holding one wrinkly hand over the knight's forehead while removing a dagger from the man's belly with the other. She lithely pushed herself off the horse and scurried into the forest. Victor fell and hit the ground while trying to push his innards back inside his body.

A furious roar nearly knocked the lords off their horses and forced Otto to step back from the brambles. He spotted an animal's furry face, unlike any he'd ever seen: black, beady eyes that looked strangely human but couldn't be; and a mashed, crooked nose and mouth, out of which sprang curved yellow teeth. And the putrid smell!

"Ride!" Fear cracked Otto's voice as he remounted his horse, waiting for his masters to bolt ahead of him.

One lord galloped away while the second prepared to follow, but before he could, the old woman jumped from the woods, landing in front of the horse and letting forth an ear-splitting screech, causing the animal to rear high on its hind legs. As it did, the woman drew two curved blades from behind her back and swiftly slit a bloody X on the horse's belly. The animal's scream prickled the lord's hair. The lord thought quickly, and instead of tumbling, pushed himself off the horse and landed on his feet as the beast collapsed forward and onto the ground, writhing in pain along with Victor. The lord ran to Otto, placed both hands on Hans's back and propelled himself upward to sit behind Otto and *on* the dead knight. Otto's horse ran for its life.

The old woman stowed her weapons and scrambled into the woods to chase the lords and knight.

The thing that had roared at Otto rose from the brambles and strode into the road near the dying horse and Victor, who had stopped squirming and rested on his side as offal oozed through his fingers. He looked up to see a horned monster holding a chain in one hand and a strange bundle of sticks, wielded like a club, in the other.

"You've been good, Herr Knight, but nothing can save your life now—only end your misery." It lifted a cloven hoof, balancing itself on the other, and crushed Victor's head, offering him a surprisingly quick death.

It took two stomps to kill the horse.

Chapter Five

Although Beate Klothilda had been to the Vettelberg Castle earlier that day with Heinrich, she'd previously visited the palace only a handful of times, mostly with Gisela—she considered her friend a superior seamstress and always would—to help sell her wares to visiting nobles or castle workers. But even during those few precious times, she had been relegated to a meager, hastily erected tent fronting the inner curtain walls that protected the great hall and keep—never had she been inside to see its true grandeur.

"The baron is spending the conclusion of Twelfth Night in upper Bavaria," said Mumfred, the castle steward who led Beate along the outer courtyard's cobblestone path to the inner castle's gatehouse. "It's actually fortuitous that he is. Otherwise the castle would be a madhouse of baking, planning for festivities and so forth. Meaning we'd have to keep an eye on you to make sure nothing goes missing."

Beate caught a glimpse of Heinrich balling his fists. She squeezed his forearm to calm him.

She knew not to escalate things. "I can assure you nothing of the sort will happen."

Mumfred led the group, including two squires on the verge of knighthood, to the inner gatehouse's entrance, where guards began lifting its smaller but no less imposing portcullis.

Beate took the moment to feast upon the gothic castle's size. The four outer curtain walls, constructed of gray stone and mortar, loomed ninety feet over anyone who approached the castle—after somehow traversing the moat oozing around its perimeter.

Those four walls, each four hundred feet long and topped with battlements, formed a square, with one-hundred-and-twenty-feet-tall rectangular, spire-topped bastions serving as the castle's corners. Guards, looking outward and down the mountain, paced the wall walks. Standing at an inner curtain wall base, Beate gazed upward, spotting two guards looking down at her. They too stood atop a ninety-foot-tall wall. However, the four walls on which they were perched measured two hundred feet long—creating a small fortress encased by a larger one. And even though the inner and outer walls stood the same height if placed side by side, the inner structures, because they were built on a taller point on the mountain, rose higher.

"Remove your dagger." Mumfred pleasantly extended his hand to Heinrich. "I'm surprised our squires didn't think to ask you first."

Mumfred smirked at the two blushing boys—for that's all they were—who shot embarrassed glances at each other.

"I suppose that's why they're still squires." Mumfred accepted the sheathed weapon and performed impromptu pat-downs on both Heinrich and Beate. "I believe Otto already did this, but one can never be too careful."

Mumfred noticed Heinrich's displeasure as he took his time frisking Beate.

"Now you know why I took this from you." He jiggled the dagger. "The porter shall return this to you when you leave. Follow me."

As they walked, Mumfred directed the peasants to view a cluster of small, square apartments constructed in stone against an outer curtain wall's interior side.

"You've already passed the seamstress's quarters. I'm not sure which it is, but she lives—or used to—in one of them. Perhaps if you please the baroness with your work—because, really, decisions of this nature are hers to make—you can dwell there."

Beate dreamed of one day living in the castle full time, sewing exotic materials into clothes for its master. But that dream died upon meeting Mumfred.

"Or I could continue to live in the village." She smiled at the steward, making sure he noticed.

"A village life over one in a castle?" Mumfred dismissed the idea with a grunt. "You jest."

"Me? Jesting?" She said it innocently. "No, I'm certain the castle already has a fool."

Heinrich and the two squires fought to suppress laughter. Mumfred furrowed his brow. "Just because you're a guest of one of the baron's sons doesn't mean you're under the boy's protection. *I* run the castle when the baron's not here. Do you understand me?"

Beate held her tongue and curtsied.

"Whatever. Come." Mumfred waved them to follow. "Seeing that we cannot expect either of the two lords to set foot into the seamstress's dwelling, you'll be sizing them in their sleeping quarters within the solar."

Beate's heart fluttered upon entering the inner courtyard. People from miles away could see the bergfried's churn tower, but to see it now, jutting more than one hundred and seventy-five feet in the air.

"We'll be going up there?" She marveled at the circular tower's four bartizans, each with a conical top. Those four outposts encircled a tower, smaller in diameter, that served as the entire structure's spire.

Mumfred chuckled. "Silly girl, that's the tower of last resort. I don't expect barbarian hordes to mount a siege while the baron is away, but that's where he'd be if one happened. Knowing the baron, he'd go down fighting. No, the baron and his family live in a palas in one of the lower, separate structures." He pointed to what Beate had never accurately seen from outside the castle: an ornate five-story building with several curved archways and windows fronting the bergfried.

"That's where you'll find the main hall and solar, and the baron's sons—eventually," Mumfred said. "And that's where we're going for your meal."

They were about to enter when Otto's booming voice caused them to turn.

"Raise it, raise the damn thing now." It came from a distance away.

"He means the front gatehouse. Follow me, no straying." Mumfred led the way to the outer courtyard and the main entrance, where the gate began rising.

Knights rushed the wall walks from above and pointed through the battlements to two horses galloping toward the lowered drawbridge. The animals, pushed to their limits by their masters, practically ripped wood from the bridge as they crossed into the castle.

Everyone dismounted. Wilhelm and Karl stood next to each other underneath the spiked gate and drew their bows, waiting for whatever had ruthlessly attacked three knights and two horses to appear. Archers atop the castle walls likewise aimed long and crossbows.

The commotion stirred Heinrich, Beate, Mumfred, the squires and numerous other castle denizens to linger behind the lords, soon filling the archway with gawkers.

Unknown to everyone, two sets of eyes bored through the dense woods. An old woman stayed in the forest to the right of the path leading to the castle, and a monster hid within the fauna to the road's left.

Otto took control. "My lords, lower your bows, get inside the castle, now." He then stood on the drawbridge's hinges, making sure everyone inside the castle could see him. "Now step back!"

Nobody argued with the giant knight. They backtracked as Otto menacingly marched forward to hammer home the point. Once he was safely out of range of the spikes: "Lower the gate, raise the drawbridge!"

Everyone milling behind the descending gate heard from within the woods what sounded like a man and a woman arguing—loudly—followed by metal clashing against metal, then two distinct beings howling and screeching at each other.

Beate hugged Heinrich, who watched the closed gate and drawbridge as if there was still something to see outside.

"Love." She waited for him to meet her eyes. "I think we're staying here tonight."

Chapter Six

"Whoever you are—or *what*ever you are—you're severely hindering my efforts to rid the world of one its most deviant miscreants." The old woman lurched out of the forest, this time without her pail and sack. She slashed the air with her two knives, preparing herself. "I suggest you step out where I can see you. That's *my* prize in the castle, and I'll be damned if some, some, I don't know, *werewolf* is going to claim him."

"Werewolf?" Deep laughter came from the other side of the forest, and what the old lady had first mistaken for twisted tree branches—long, jagged animal horns—rose from a bramble patch, followed by the eight-foot-tall hairy beast from which they jutted.

"Do you see a full moon? I don't," the thing said. "And since when do werewolves run around on hooves?" The creature, holding its chain and club, lifted one of its hooves to show the woman.

"Ah, I've indeed heard of you," the woman said. "At least I *think* you're Saint Nicholas's errand boy."

"Nice to meet you, Frau Perchta." The beast exaggeratedly bowed. "The master knows this is your territory and your time of year."

The thing dropped its chain, but not its club, to let its massive barrel slip off its back. It used one hoof to push the barrel off the road while simultaneously stooping to retrieve the long chain. The hag and the beast assessed each other as they began circling clockwise, twenty feet separating them.

"Then what on earth are you doing here *now*?" Perchta said. "You and the saint had your day last month. I'm on my twelfth and final one, and this particular brat is proving a lot more troublesome than I'd anticipated."

"You cannot seriously believe that I can snatch everybody that my master assigns me in *one* day? Especially when the mark is out of town. Even I need to eat breakfast, lunch and dinner. And the occasional deer snack. And I'm not immune to when nature calls. I suppose I could wait until next year, but some of the wretches do not deserve the luxury of time to commit more of their misdeeds. That's why I'm here, now, with the mark in that castle."

"That's *my* mark," Perchta said in a raised voice, and shook one of her knives at the monster. "I've distributed the coins I planned on giving today, and took care of one of the two brats who deserved it. One more to go—or two. I've yet to decide."

"No. I've been eyeing this kid for months. And I'm not about to let some withered shrew screw it up."

"Withered? Shrew?" She let the insult linger and looked at her feet, appearing hurt. Then she sprang toward the monster, spinning like a cyclone, her two blades slashing deep gashes into the surprised creature's belly. She landed and kicked the monster onto its back.

The thing whipped its chain around Perchta's right wrist and yanked. Bones cracked and she released the dagger, which twirled into the woods. She shrieked and doubled over in pain as the monster pushed itself off the ground and charged the woman.

Perchta stooped and scurried under the horrendously smelling archway created by the monster's wide stance and used her remaining knife to slash the monster's Achilles tendons.

It howled and fell to its knees just as the woman scooted from beneath it. She rammed her blade into the creature's belly, but it was like skewering rock. She saw her two previous slice marks had begun to congeal and heal. She went to overhand stab the monster, but the thing countered by whipping the chain to divert the knife, and then smacked the woman back with its club.

Perchta withdrew and held the blade tip toward her foe.

"What are you?" she said. "How can you heal so quickly?"

It strained to stand on one wobbly leg and then the next.

"You mean how can I heal just as quickly as your wrist?" It nodded at Perchta's right hand, which otherwise looked straight and healthy, not twisted and broken.

"I know that the people we hunt cannot comprehend what they're up against once confronted," she said. "So allow me to finally understand what that truly feels like."

"I feel pain, as you do," it said. "But nobody's come close to ever stopping or eluding me. And I guarantee you that will never happen. I hear like an owl and have a hawk's vision. My eyesight will *never* fail me."

"Very well. I suppose we can fight in circles here while daylight wastes, or we can focus on what we both came here to do." She tucked the blade into her belt and took a neutral stance.

The thing responded by tossing its club and chain near its barrel on the roadside.

"And how do we do that?"

"Simple," she said. "You're up for a good fight, obviously. You enjoy competition. So here's the fairest way to settle it. First one who grabs the mark gets to punish him. I've got an entire sackful of straw that's destined for that kid's stomach."

The thing tilted its head, ruminating over the proposition. "The master has given me freedom to do what I wish with the creeps. That is enough motivation for me to snag him first. What are the parameters?"

"Do either of us *look* like we follow rules?" Perchta said.

"I tend to think I adhere to a personal code of conduct and—"

"Listen, *genius*, if you think I'm going to let you just waltz into the castle, you're insane. If I see you climbing a wall, you better expect me to throw something to stop you. You've got your chain over there. Do you think for a second I'd hesitate to use that against you?"

The creature went to answer but—

"No!" she continued. "I fully expect you to whip that thing at me if you see I'm about to be on the boy."

"I thought we weren't going to fight each other," it said.

"That's right, we're not. The front of the castle is off-limits.

That's a rule I can adhere to. You take your side of the castle and I'll take mine. We'll be too busy trying to scale the walls than to worry about foiling each other."

"Fair enough. But what about the castle's rear?"

"We split the castle in two—and not literally, genius. You have your side that will wrap halfway around to the castle's rear."

"And you'll have yours."

"Riiiiiight." She drew it out like it had two syllables, enjoying how to plot and win the game of wits and strength ahead of them. "I expect the last thing we want to do is meet in the middle behind the castle."

"Deal." The monster nodded, also feeling enlivened by the challenge. "We avoid each other, stay off each other's side. But once we're inside, anything goes."

"Agreed." She held out her claw-like right hand and the monster did likewise. She grabbed the tip of its kielbasa-sized finger and shook. "But don't you go anywhere yet. I need to find my knife."

"Yeah, my legs need to heal a little more too." It arched its back to look behind at its calf muscles to see the Achilles wounds mending by themselves.

"You and your hawk eyes could help me look for my knife, you know. It would speed things up considerably." She stepped one foot into the forest to begin her search. "By the way, what do I call you?"

It walked into the forest, eyeing her, and grunted, "Krampus."

Chapter Seven

"And you're sure he wasn't missing anything?" Mumfred examined Hans's body, which Otto had placed on the ground near the closed portcullis—and off to its side stood Heinrich, holding Beate against his body to warm her as the sun began to set.

"His crossbow, sword, he even had some coins in his saddlebag—Victor said it was all there when we found him," Otto said. Lords Wilhelm and Karl added what they could about the attack on the hunting party.

"We should fetch the bodies," Mumfred said. "If the villagers see dead knights strewn about the road, they might think the baron and his kin weak. Rumors could spread to other towns, and to our enemies. Uprisings have occurred over less."

Beate, still surrounded by several Vettelberg workers, said nothing. She stared, expressionless, at the vertical gash made down Hans's belly.

"That crone cut straight through Victor's chain mail in one clean swipe," Otto continued, trying not to let on that he wanted no part in retrieving bodies. "I'm not sure *I* could pull off something like that. This hunchbacked woman, the way she moved. The feeble only move that fast when they drop dead. They don't hop on horses and then disembowel them. And I still don't know what wielded that chain. It couldn't have been the woman. I'm guessing a marauder dressed in multiple furs, wearing war paint. But I'm not even convinced of that."

Mumfred, taller than everyone except Otto, addressed the young lords. "I believe the baron would impale me if I allowed you two to set foot from this castle until we have a better handle on things. So you're staying here. And the baron must be told."

Mumfred stood on his tiptoes to scan the crowd of thirty people that had formed a semicircle around Hans and the survivors. "Where's the messenger? James, are you there?"

"I am." A lean, fit man in his twenties, James wormed his way through the people to Mumfred, who put his hand on James's shoulder.

"Go to the stables, get the fastest horse you can find." Mumfred glanced at Hans's death wound and then back to James. "Get a weapon. A dagger, something light and easy to wield. I need you to fly posthaste to inform the baron of this. Write down the names of the knights and whatever other details Otto and the lords feel sufficient and then set off. You should be able to reach the mountain's base before it gets too dark, and then it's not far to the port on the Rhine. Take the river until you reach Mannheim and its castle, and inform the baron."

"With all respect, it's obviously dangerous out there and—"

Mumfred pressed two fingers against James's lips to shush him. The young messenger could not help but constantly glance at Hans's body.

"I realize I'm volunteering you for a suicide mission. All I'm asking is you ride your horse to the port—not the Mannheim castle. You can do it. Stop for nobody. Dress warmly. The sun's setting fast. *Go!*"

James sprinted to his quarters to prepare for the journey while Mumfred stared at the hushed crowd.

"I suggest all of you return to your duties, whatever they may be. If you live in the village—" Mumfred specifically addressed Beate and Heinrich but spoke loud enough so that other villagers could hear, "—then we will find shelter for you tonight."

"*Really?*" It was Wilhelm.

"Young master," Mumfred said. "We wouldn't want the rest of the villagers to know that we forced their loved ones to travel dangerous paths while keenly aware that brutal killers lay in wait for them."

"Just make sure they clean up after themselves," Wilhelm said. "Now on to more important matters. I'm famished." He surveyed the crowd and smiled. "Boris, what have you prepared for me?"

The housekeeper, a portly, profusely sweaty man of thirty whose cheeks flushed red, not out of embarrassment but because the kitchen was hot, stood in the gaggle's rear.

"Per Lord Karl's instructions, in honor of his guests, tonight the cooks have prepared roast duck, assorted vegetables and breads. It will be served at your leisure."

"Splendid." Mumfred clapped his hands. "My lords, after you."

"I'll take my meal in my chambers, if you please." Wilhelm turned to the second gateway leading to the hall.

"I'll sit with *our* guests," Karl countered.

"*You* invited them. I'll be ready for my fitting once they're done gorging their little bellies." Wilhelm glanced over his shoulder toward Beate as he walked. "You will thoroughly wash your hands." And he was gone.

The assemblage of curious castle workers and residents dwindled. Atop his horse, James, the messenger, dressed in a woolen tunic and cloak for warmth, rode from the stables situated at the far side of the outer courtyard.

"Don't leave yet," Mumfred said and turned to Franco, the castle burgmann, who'd kept quiet but monitored the entire situation. "I want some of your best riders to escort him to the point where the bodies should be. Bring them back. Be on guard."

"It will take but a minute to prepare." A white-bearded warrior in his forties who oversaw castle security turned to Otto, who served as his second-in-command. "I'll take care of the riders. Get some sentries to line the drawbridge when our men leave. I don't want anyone charging his way into this castle."

Otto nodded and left.

"Beate and Heinrich, please follow me to the great hall." Mumfred cordially extended his arm.

"What about him?" Beate pointed to Hans, his lifeless eyes still open.

"You need not worry. I don't believe this knight was married, so that certainly saves us the grief of informing a wife. Now come. I do want the lords fitted beginning this evening. And you." Mumfred addressed Heinrich. "I know you're a skilled blacksmith, and you're quite aware of the opening here. We'll see what you can do tomorrow to perhaps earn you an extended stay. The baron will make the final decision, naturally. But since he's not here, why not try you out?"

Heinrich smiled and looked at Beate, who beamed.

"What would you need, sir?" Heinrich said.

Mumfred waved over two stable boys who were escorting two knights' horses to the front gatehouse. "After the knights leave, find a place to store this poor fellow." Mumfred motioned to Hans. "Be dignified about it. We'll bury him someplace tomorrow."

The boys nodded and avoided eye contact.

"Now, as for what we'll need." Mumfred stroked his chin. "Based on current events, I would say weapons."

Chapter Eight

The drawbridge abruptly clanked downward. No sooner had the fifty-foot-long plank covered the moat than eight guards—four on each side, brandishing broadswords and pikes—lined the bridge. They scanned all directions, waiting for a possible onslaught. The setting sun provided enough light to see.

A knight on horseback charged across the bridge to the road leading down the mountain. James followed on his horse, keeping pace, and was trailed by a second knight on his steed. The guards watched for sudden movements from either side of the forest as the riders approached the woods.

The drumbeat of hooves abated, and no sound or sight indicated the horsemen ran afoul of anything.

Frau Perchta and Krampus took positions within the woods, on opposite sides of the road leading to the castle. Neither paid mind to the riders once they confirmed their mark wasn't on horseback.

The only rule—proposed by Perchta and agreed upon by Krampus—was that the castle's front was off-limits to both.

Perchta immediately disregarded it and reached for her knee-high boots, on which were four small sheaths sewn vertically along the leather.

The eight guards had begun their cautious retreat into the barbican when, to a man, each heard two metal chinks, one right after the other.

"Hold up!" Otto had heard it too and muscled his way

through the eight guards and stood immediately behind the bridge's pivots, looking outward, seeing nothing but a distant red sun. He called over his shoulder, "Any of you hit? Wounded?"

Murmurings of *no* came in reply.

He stepped back to make sure he was clear of the portcullis's spikes.

"Raise the drawbridge! Lower the gate!"

The thick iron chains lining each side of the bridge jerked upward but halted, as did the portcullis spikes hanging overhead.

Otto looked up. "Drop it!" He knew the portcullis was built so that when it lowered, the drawbridge would automatically rise.

"It won't move!" came a voice from within the castle.

Otto drew his broadsword, holding it in one hand like a machete. He crept onto the bridge, ready to jump back in case the gate suddenly dropped. He looked up to see slim, flat objects wedged within the link of each chain leading directly into the bridge's pulleys, concealed behind ornamental stone circles.

"Oh my God," Otto said.

He heard flitting air before feeling his flesh sting. He fell to a knee and grunted and then fumbled to remove the small knife jutting from his neck near the trapezius muscle—a spot unguarded by chain mail. He plucked out a metal throwing knife and realized two of the exact same blades were preventing the chains from entering the castle, keeping the bridge down. He then heard a screech and she was upon him.

He dropped his sword and began swatting at her, his hands and arms protected by thick leather gloves and iron gauntlets. It looked like he was giving a piggyback ride to his attacker, who repeatedly plunged a long knife into him, striking metal and not desired skin.

The woman dug her boot heels into his sides and wrapped her left arm around his head, trying to wrench it sideways to find a meaty spot to stab. Otto reached for his sword on the bridge, but the old woman yanked his head in the opposite direction, causing him to stumble toward the castle.

Otto, who'd tucked his chin to his chest to better surround

his vulnerable neck with chain mail, backhanded the woman's face. Undeterred, she tightened her grip and swiped the dagger across his cheek, unleashing a hot, bloody spray.

The knight screamed and knew he needed help removing this tick of a woman. He barreled into the castle and stood in the middle of the barbican hallway leading to the gatehouse. "Shoot! Shoot, damn you!"

Arrows darted from loops spaced along the passage's walls. While many clattered off stone, one arrow slipped through the woman's ribs, and another jutted from her back. She screamed a mix of pain and fury.

Only a few guards needed to defend the barbican: two on each side and two above. Anyone who stormed the castle would need to get through the portcullis, enter the barbican and then breach the gatehouse door to actually enter the castle's courtyard. In the meantime they were easy prey for the barbican's guards, who hid behind the walls and fired arrows through the loopholes. And that was only one method of defense.

Otto knew this and positioned his back toward the loopholes, giving the guards clear shots. Pretty soon the woman's back resembled a porcupine's in reverse. She dropped from Otto, who tumbled toward the gatehouse door, screaming "Now!"

The guards posted on the barbican's roof made sure the big knight was clear. They always kept a caldron of boiling oil at the ready just in case someone attempted a siege. Finally they had a chance to use it. The two guards, their hands protected in leather, pushed the huge pot forward, tipping its gruesome black brew through a grating and splattering it onto Perchta, who was straining to yank arrows from her back. She squealed as the oil poured into every crevice it could find. She ran from the barbican and stopped on the drawbridge, the combined pain of the arrows and oil compelling her to pluck a few more from her body before making a full retreat.

Otto burst from the barbican and shouldered into her, but it was like tackling a mountain. He bounced off and sat before her, confused and then fearful because of the arrow that she pointed an inch from his eye. All she needed to do was poke it forward to skewer his brain. How she'd composed herself enough to do this, while covered with burning oil and still resembling a pincushion, eluded Otto, but he did not cower and accepted his fate.

"I'm getting in that castle, and I will walk over your dead body to do it," she seethed through gritted teeth.

She had brought back the bloody arrow just enough to drive it home when a thick black chain smashed sideways into her ribs, knocking her off the drawbridge, sending her screaming into the moat below.

Instead of looking at a fearsome, malevolent hag, Otto now faced a giant, hairy devil standing at the foot of the drawbridge.

"She cheated," was all it said before whipping the chain at both pulleys and one by one knocking the throwing knives away from the links, freeing the drawbridge of obstruction.

Otto, still sitting, kicked himself toward the castle and into the barbican, clear of the portcullis, and watched the rising wooden plank conceal the indescribable creature opposite the moat.

Chapter Nine

"What I find most amusing about the castle are the toilets," Mumfred said to Beate and Heinrich, both of whom sat at one of the many long wooden trestle tables in the great hall, feasting on roast duck.

The young lovebirds glanced at each other, not sure why the steward would direct the dinner conversation in this way.

"I say that because I'm not sure how you peasants manage to live near your own waste, but the baron's engineers devised it so that all of the castle's twenty toilets flow directly into the moat. And the holes are cut small enough—and the toilets situated high enough off the ground—so that invaders cannot crawl their way inside." He smiled, expecting the filthy images they would surely conjure to sap their appetites.

Beate gulped her duck. "And all this while I thought that smell came from some of the people who escorted us into the castle."

"Ha!" Lord Karl walked behind Mumfred and clapped him on the back hard enough that the steward wobbled forward and made the table's candle flames dance. "Good one, maiden. This place could use a little levity, given all that has transpired." Karl turned to the steward. "Mummy, surely your position requires you to be mindful of other castle matters and not to follow around these good people of the village to make sure they don't pocket the silverware."

Mumfred scowled at Beate, fuming that Karl's intervention prevented him from reaming out the snippy peasant. "My lord, when you and your brother are ready to be fitted, please summon me and I shall arrange to have these two escorted to your—"

"That won't be necessary." Karl sat across from Beate and Heinrich with a plate of duck and vegetables and waved off Mumfred. "I'll take care of things myself. Have some faith that everyone who enters the castle isn't the scoundrel you suspect them to be."

Mumfred huffed away. Beate paid him no mind and marveled that a good chunk of the village—including its buildings—could stand inside the hall. She guessed it to measure one hundred and fifty feet long and seventy feet wide, with the hammer-beam ceiling at least that tall.

"Normally I'd be sitting on the dais." Karl glanced at a raised platform supporting a table at the far end of the hall. "But the baron is absent, as are other nobles. I don't view it as slumming to be seen eating with peasants. My brother is a different story." Karl waited for Heinrich and Beate to say something—then realized why they hadn't. "You've never actually been inside the castle before, have you?"

"No, my lord," Beate said while looking at one of the many tapestries depicting knights atop horses during battle that lined the hall's walls. Elsewhere were shields adorned with the baron's coat of arms. Five fireplaces, some so large that people could walk into them, heated the room. A row of stained-glass windows stretched across the top of a long wall, allowing for sunshine to occasionally light the dais.

"Castle living isn't all that it's made out to be, I can assure you," Karl said in between mouthfuls of carrots. "It's cold, damp and dark most of the time. Using torches to walk around at night does nothing but clog the hallways with smoke."

"But it's safe here, my lord," Beate said. "After seeing what happened to Gisela—my friend—that could not happen within these walls."

"The castle is its own little city, Beate—if I may be so bold." Karl looked to Heinrich.

"It's her name, my lord."

"As I was saying, the castle's work staff, when fully thrumming, exceeds two hundred, at the least. When the baron entertains, you'll see dozens of cooks in the kitchen. You'll see bottlers and butlers. And that's just for providing food. The castle has its own carpenters, its own chaplain. Armorers—the blacksmith, you should know!" Karl motioned to Heinrich.

"Of course."

"My point is we try to find the most honest people we can to work here. Many live in the village, many in the castle. But they're not all saints. Jealousy, greed, envy—they don't exclusively exist outside of the castle, waiting to breach the walls to corrupt its denizens. Immorality sleeps wherever man lays a pillow. I'm not trying to say that living in a castle is no better than in a hut. Clearly that's bunk. Sometimes castles protect bad people from evil ones. But you still wouldn't want anything to do with either of them."

Beate gulped water from a goblet, finishing it. "My lord, respectfully, I'm not calling your brother evil or bad."

"He's bad," Karl interjected.

"Very well." She spoke cautiously. "That was the feeling I got when he viewed Gisela as an unpleasant mess rather than a murdered woman. What I'm saying is your father is a fair man to the peasants. What happens in the event that your brother succeeds him?"

"My father is aware of my brother's unkindness and what that might mean for the villagers and surrounding lords. The baron doesn't seek to expand his reach. He's content with what he has, and that has been instilled in us. And just in case the baron's not here, he's made it explicitly clear that Mumfred calls the shots—not Wilhelm."

Heinrich devoured his duck to bones, tired of the current conversation. "Your wedding, my lord. I promise you Beate will tailor you a fine outfit."

"I don't doubt that, but if I may be so bold as to pull rank, my impending nuptials are not something I care to discuss. Let us just say I vehemently disagree with arranged marriages."

Beate finished her plate and pushed it toward the middle of the table. "Your brother is married, correct, my lord? How does he view it?"

Karl rolled his eyes. "My brother and his wife are a perfect fit. They care not a wit about each other and neither gets upset about it. Each goes behind the other's back at will. They dress nicely and show up at galas to keep up appearances, but beyond that, it's a sham—what I fully expect my marriage to be. You two are lucky."

Beate reached under the table and squeezed Heinrich's hand.

"Now then, I see you are finished," Karl said. "And I do not presume to rush your beau. So, please, Heinrich, stay here and eat while Beate fits me. I promise not to keep her long, and we will arrange to have you both sheltered here this evening." He turned to Beate. "Your friend, Gisela, she made good headway on my brother's outfit, so how about you get the unpleasant part out of the way and do what needs to be done to him, and then me? Is that acceptable?"

"It is. Thank you, my lord."

"And if he displays his obnoxious side to the point of you wanting to strike him—and that likely will happen—I'd advise you to not strike him, but simply leave the room. My chamber is across the hall from his, and you may retreat there if you feel threatened. And I mean that."

"Thank you, my lord." This time it was Heinrich.

"Follow me, Beate." He smiled and began walking to exit the hall when Otto barreled in, panting.

"My lord, a devil prevented a witch from killing me."

Chapter Ten

Inside the great hall, everyone—from the servers and scullions scuttling in and out of the kitchen to the chaplain seated at a table parallel to Beate's—stared at the huffing knight, who realized all eyes were on him.

"Otto, please, sit down." Karl walked Otto to an empty table to seat him and then waved a servant to bring food and drink. The young lord grabbed a cloth napkin and pressed it against Otto's bloody cheek. Otto took the cloth and kept the pressure steady. By this time, Lord Wilhelm had arrived from his chamber to see what was delaying his fitting. Noticing the commotion around Otto, Wilhelm joined his brother. "What happened to you?"

Otto recounted everything. "I am not hallucinating. I have not partaken of too much drink. What the woman did to me was real and witnessed by guards in the barbican."

"Did anyone else see the devil?" Wilhelm's incredulousness drew looks from around the room. Mumfred reentered and joined the nobles.

"Perhaps guards on the wall walks," Otto said. "My lords, both of you need bodyguards around you at all times."

"Pish, Otto," Wilhelm said. "The castle's defenses held up just as designed. Post extra guards up top. Oh, and get one of the cottars to fish the woman out of the moat."

"I would not do that, my lord, lest you wish the cottar dead." The chaplain, a man named Theodore, stood. "And I would suggest you follow the knight's suggestion about bodyguards."

Wilhelm rolled his eyes and sighed. "Loosen your robe, priest. It's on too tight."

Theodore, a cherub of a man, flapped his long brown and white robes. "They are fine. What I am suggesting, my lord, is that the woman the knight described likely already is out of the moat—and angry to have been knocked in there in the first place by Krampus."

"Excuse me?" It was Mumfred. Beate followed him to stand near the chaplain. Heinrich remained seated, surreptitiously poking duck in his mouth.

"The thing the knight described. That's Krampus. The dark servant to Saint Nicholas. But what he's doing out of his cave this time of year—"

"Too much red wine, Father," Mumfred said. "Perhaps you need to skip evening Mass."

"On the coming of the Epiphany?" Theodore walked to where Otto sat. "I think not, my lord. And that explains the woman who attacked the knight. It's Frau Perchta. I've heard stories of her comings and goings in Bavaria, but never have I seen her, nor do I wish to."

"I cannot blame you." Otto grunted. "She was too strong to be—"

"What did her feet look like?" Theodore said.

Otto looked up, rolling his eyes back and forth, thinking. "One of them was odd, deformed, by the look of her boot."

"Like a goose's foot?"

"I didn't think of it that way, Father, but it was flat."

"My lords." Theodore stood before the brothers and placed a hand on each man's shoulder to huddle. "Every conceivable entrance of this castle must be fortified for the foreseeable future. At least until the Twelfth Night festivities have long passed. She won't let up. Not until she guts and sews up whoever she's after."

"What?" Beate's voice echoed around the hall.

"Wait a minute," Wilhelm said, his irreverence slipped to concern.

"That woman we put on Hans's horse." Otto stood and pointed to Beate. "That girl's friend."

"She was murdered in such a manner, Father," Beate said. "Her body was defiled and left on the roadside." Beate recounted what she'd seen.

"The seamstress," Theodore recalled. "I remember seeing her around here." He shook his head to refocus. "Then, my dear, I regret to tell you that your friend must have done something the frau frowns upon. Perhaps she didn't meet her quota of spun wool?"

Wilhelm arched an eyebrow. "This Frau Perchta worries about how much people sew?"

"Yes, according to the tales I've read. Her goose foot resembles a splayfoot that works a spinning-woman's treadle. So perhaps she does. Or it marks that she's some other type of being, a higher power, a spirit of nature and defender of the woodlands. And she also frowns upon people *not* eating fish during Twelfth Night in favor of something else. Perhaps it's an old superstition of mine, but that's why I requested the cooks prepare me some salmon. It was good too."

Everyone else within earshot looked at their dinner plates holding an assortment of ravaged duck carcasses. Heinrich slowly gulped the last bit of poultry in his mouth and released the leg bone, which landed on a metal plate with a deadening thump.

"Again, just a superstition," Theodore said.

"And this Krampus? The devil my father spoke of to us as children to scare us?" Wilhelm said. "Saint Nicholas's brutish right hand that absconds with naughty children every December fifth to torture them? *That's* the man who knocked Perchta in the moat?"

"My lord, it was no man," Otto said. "It had hooves for feet, a tail, Horns that were part of no costume. Nothing in this world has ever scared me. Not until tonight. That *thing* did."

"Then perhaps this Krampus fellow should invest in a calendar because he's a month behind schedule," Wilhelm said. "The Eve of Saint Nicholas has long since past. The people in the village—even a few in the castle—who dress as the beast on that night and partake in drink and merriment have put their costumes away for next year. Maybe one of them is a little overzealous or still eats off of lead plates."

Nobody replied to the elder brother. "Now then, I'm tired of this nonsense and wish to be fitted—girl, Beate—accompany me please. Hopefully this won't take too long."

Wilhelm made a beeline for the exit. Beate kissed Heinrich on the cheek. "Stay in here, please. Don't venture outside."

"Watch out for yourself." He looked to make sure Wilhelm had gone. "I don't trust him."

"Nor I." Beate scampered to catch up to Wilhelm, but Karl waited by the exit to accompany her.

"It was real." Otto straightened himself and walked to leave the hall. All eyes looked at him. "Whether you believe me or not."

Chapter Eleven

The wall walk archers lit extra torches lining the castle's front curtain wall and poked their heads between the battlement crenels to scour the moat.

"Lots of good the torches do us up here," Franco, the castle's burgmann and best bowman, said before spitting a gob of tobacco in the moat. "We can see shit up here but none of the shit down *there*."

"Maybe the moonlight will help." Otto, his neck and cheek wounds salved with a mix of yarrow and myrrh and bandaged in linen, gazed at a white moon illuminating the castle in a silver glow—only to be dimmed by hulking black clouds drifting across the sky.

"Let's get on with it then," Franco said. "Archers, draw!"

Twenty-four archers stretched across the wall walk, two to a crenel, aimed at all parts of the moat. "Lower the bridge!" Franco yelled.

The wooden door yawned to a stop and out scurried four cottars, the lowest-ranking castle employees—each with a torch in one shaky hand, a pike in the other. They spread out, lowering the torches to the moat to look for a floating body.

"Three men up here witnessed that thing whipping the hag into the moat," Franco told Otto. "They've not taken their eyes off the spot where she splashed down. She went under and did not come out."

Vettelberg Castle was specifically built atop a massive rock surrounded by an O-shaped ditch that made for a natural moat. A mix of water and waste filled half of the twenty-foot-deep ditch, whose edges stood ten feet above the murk's surface, making it near impossible for attackers to pull themselves up and out. Even if they managed to escape on the castle's side of the moat, they had only ten feet of rocky space to maneuver, nowhere near enough room to queue forces.

The cottars, whose duties included removing waste from the moat when the stench became too powerful, now dipped their heads uncomfortably close to the watery filth, hoping, praying they could somehow see a body that could be pulled out with pikes.

"Could she have swum around, maybe snuck out on another side of the castle?" Otto said.

"We've been watching all sides of the castle—we'd have seen her," Franco said.

"Then she's down there."

One cottar, dressed in a ragged tunic not warm enough for the cold, handed his torch to a fellow flunky, who dropped his pike to hold two torches. The first cottar stuck his long pike into the moat, poking around, jabbing for the hag.

"Work your way right to circle the castle," Franco called to them. "We'll keep watch on the areas you've covered."

They wordlessly acquiesced and continued their dirty work.

"If your men saw the hag fall into the moat, then they certainly saw what sent her there," Otto said.

Franco, watching the cottars while addressing Otto, knew not to be flippant with the giant knight for fear that doing so would mean joining the hag at the moat's bottom.

"This devil-man with the chain, yes—he turned tail and retreated for the forest. We've not seen him since."

"Do you believe me? Do your men believe what they saw?"

"My men witnessed something that was somehow bigger than you whip that witch into that mire. I can't say *what* exactly they saw because I wasn't present. I don't doubt that you saw a man covered with furs."

"Then why the antlers, the horns?" Otto said.

"I've got something!" one of the cottars yelled, sparing Franco from having to answer.

"What is it?" the burgmann said.

"A body, it must be!" answered Fritz, the cottar whose pike

touched on something soft and lumpy. While his long weapon had a spear tip, it also featured a sharp hook curved toward the wielder. Fritz fidgeted the hook to snag clothing or a rib or a sturdy body part.

The young cottar gulped when the mass jiggled the prodding pike tip. The three remaining cottars joined Fritz. Two held torches while the third man used his pike to help Fritz hook and haul.

The hook caught hold of something.

"Got it," Fritz said. *Maybe I looped the hook under the armpit?* he thought. He tightened his grip and stepped backward, straining to lift the mass to surface.

Fritz inhaled, his jaw trembling. Whatever he'd snagged squeezed the pike's shaft and jerked it into the moat. The other men saw him lurch forward.

"Don't be such a bed wetter!" Fritz heard the jibe from above. "It's an old woman! Lift her, damn it!"

"Maybe it's a snake," Fritz said. The cottars noticed a quiver in his voice. "Yes, a snake has slithered around the pole, upset that I'm taking away its dinner."

The torchlight illuminating where the pole breached the murk showed only slight ripples as Fritz tried easing up his catch. Then the pole spasmed.

"It's alive!"

The archers—a few of the nervous ones, anyway—released arrows into the moat.

"Hold your fire!" Franco said, and then to the second pike-wielding cottar, "Help him!"

The second man dropped his weapon and grabbed part of Fritz's pike. Now the two men played tug–of–war with the unseen. But both felt the bending and crunching of wood, and then they fell backward, bringing with them a broken pike, the spear and hook snapped from the shaft.

She exploded from the moat and corkscrewed to send filth in every direction, to repulse whoever it hit. She eyed the cottars at her apex and threw the pike's blade into Fritz's diaphragm. He collapsed, grotesquely gasping, while the other three cottars retreated across drawbridge for the castle's protection. Perchta landed opposite the castle, next to Fritz's writhing body. She glowered at the bewildered archers aiming at her. Brown sludge oozed its way down her face's wrinkles, filling them like water down dry river arteries.

"Fire!"

Arrows flitted toward her throat and stomach, but she was too quick and bolted toward the forest.

"Your castle will fall!" she shrieked. And was gone.

The archers looked at where their arrows had accidentally finished off Fritz and couldn't comprehend how quickly the old woman had moved.

"Raise the drawbridge!" Franco ordered.

Every guard, regardless of their stations along the wall walks or in the castle proper, turned toward the commotion.

The monster had counted on that. He hid in a grove near the castle's side, where the darkest shadow had been cast, and ran the moment the guards glanced toward the sounds of a screaming woman bent on destroying Vettelberg.

Chapter Twelve

"Try not to touch me."

"Trust me, my lord, I'm trying not to." Beate used an ell rod to approximate the lengths required to size Lord Wilhelm's outfit for his brother's wedding.

"Your friend already measured my breeches and surcoat, so I imagine the tunic will not be much different."

"It should not, my lord." Beate recorded the measurements on parchment, trying not to feel Wilhelm staring at her the entire time they were in his bedchamber. His personal servants had layered his bed with an array of lace, silks, velvets and furs.

"Can you stitch the baron's coat of arms onto the surcoat? In gold lace?"

"I've done similar work with less expensive material." As much as Beate abhorred being so close to Wilhelm, she appreciated the warmth of his chambers, alight with candles on tabletops and hanging lanterns. The castle's hallways provided no sanctuary from the cold, and she imagined Lord Karl's chambers offered similar comfort.

She wrote down a few more measurements and said, relieved, "I have everything I need, my lord."

"You have my mother's preferences regarding materials, some of which you see in this room. Do not get ideas about swiping any of it, as we have accounted for everything and will compare it with the amount of material you use and the remaining scraps. Your friend did such a splendid job with the baron's wardrobe that he gave her a fox-fur coat. So generous, the baron."

That explains that, Beate thought. "If it is all right with you, my lord, may I begin the actual sewing tomorrow after fitting your brother?"

"That's fine. You may take up in the deceased seamstress's shack. We've cleared out everything. You might be able to sleep in an actual bed this evening and for the foreseeable future. Gisela was destined for that until her mishap."

Beate stood, her contempt unveiled. "She was murdered, my lord—births of certain people are mishaps."

Wilhelm backhanded her, and before she could recover, he pushed her against the stone wall and moved his ungloved hand up her dress, caressing her bare thigh. He whispered into Beate's ear, "It's my understanding Gisela didn't object to this treatment. Now leave."

He backed away and pointed to the door. Flushed, she hastily packed her sewing kit, grabbed the ell rod, and unlatched and pulled open the heavy wooden door. Karl stood in his chamber's open doorway and took notice of a distraught Beate stumbling out.

"Please, come in."

She rushed past him, tucked her sewing kit and ell rod under her arm, and covered her face with her hands to cry. He shut the door.

"I think I know what happened." Karl stood on his bare feet, his chain mail removed, wearing a sleeveless gray linen tunic.

"Your brother."

"Yes, it's been known to happen. And I wish it hadn't." He stood behind her and gently laid his hand on her bouncing shoulder.

"My lord, I'll lose memory of it if I work—at least I'll try. May we please?" She faced him, her red cheeks slicked with tears.

Karl placed his other hand on her, as if holding her steady. "No."

"I'm sorry?"

He squeezed her shoulders and pushed her backward, forcing her toward his bed. She turned to see it layered with nothing but blankets—no fabrics. Karl lifted and plopped her on the bed, her sewing kit bouncing next to her. He slithered atop her, forcing her legs to splay with his knees.

"I'd have preferred Wilhelm to have behaved, but urges get the better of us more times than not." He kissed up and down her neck, forced his hand up her dress and cupped her breast. He covered her mouth with his other hand to stifle the expected scream.

In between kisses and licks: "I'm surprised Wilhelm made advances. You're not really his type. Gisela, though, so innocent the first time—I regret being away for as long as I was, unable to enjoy her one last time. But you, my dear, will suffice. Tell Heinrich of this and you *will* die, as will he—in the end you're peasants, disposable and easily replaced."

Beate's thoughts varied from knowing why Karl had donned a simple tunic—she could feel his throbbing manhood brush against her as he grew aroused—to realizing one of these two cads likely was the father to Gisela's dead child. She also knew she would not be raped.

Although his weight effectively pinned her, she felt around with her right hand and skimmed the leather top of Gisela's sewing kit. She thanked God she hadn't tied it shut, and snuck her fingers between its folds. She flipped it open as Karl licked her lips. Her fingers danced over what they desired: a long bone needle. She slid it out and clenched it and boosted herself up with her elbows to return Karl's kiss, surprising him.

He momentarily eased off her, freeing her arms, and smiled. "See? What did I say about urges? You came around quicker than I thought."

"You won't like this urge." She grabbed his erect penis and drove the needle sideways, making a bloody cross.

Karl howled and sprang off the bed. Beate rose and realized her right leg was perfectly aligned. She booted his testicles and dropped him. Karl squealed as Beate yanked open the door and fled. She retraced her steps as best she could, aware that Karl's anguish likely could be heard in France.

She ran with enough speed to extinguish candles lighting the halls, and looked for a winding stairwell that led from the solar to the adjoining great hall. Spying it, she circled her way down the stairwell and burst into the great hall, where servants were lowering by chain the wooden chandelier to blow out its candles. Mumfred sat one table across from Heinrich, who drank deeply from a beer tankard. The castle steward tapped his foot, eager for the blacksmith to finish so he could be escorted to the former blacksmith's apartment, not far from the seamstress's small quarters.

Beate spotted Heinrich, who smiled and raised his mug.

"Lord Karl said we could have anything we wanted—you should try this."

She lowered his hand to set the mug on the table and spoke softly. "Get up, we must leave. Now." She grabbed both of his wrists and pulled him to stand, at which point Mumfred rose.

"Something the matter?" He circled from his table to the young couple.

Heinrich's beer intake hadn't prevented him from noticing genuine fear in Beate's eyes.

She kissed his cheek and whispered, "We're in danger. They will kill us."

He nodded and they made to leave the hall.

"I find it strange that neither Karl nor Wilhelm escorted you back, young lady." Mumfred obstructed their path. He looked at her hands clasping Heinrich's and noticed red stains. "What have you done?"

Wilhelm ran full speed into the hall and stumbled to stop. Out of breath, he pointed and glared at Beate.

"I think not." Mumfred's gangly appearance belied his strength, and he seized Beate's forearm. "Too bad your girl doesn't know her place."

Wilhelm regained enough composure to join Mumfred and grabbed Beate's shoulder from behind, only to be spooked by a deep roar of pain and hate that rattled the castle walls.

Chapter Thirteen

The guard, Kristoff, posted on the outer curtain wall walk lining the castle's left side, concealed a crossbow under a heavy bear-fur cloak. He strode by torches placed within holders on every other battlement. He couldn't see the woman from his perch halfway along the walk, but he'd heard her.

He also heard faint sounds of clip-clops, the kind made by shoed horses striding along stone. He poked his head over a crenel and saw darkness below. Had there been daylight, he'd have seen a small stone perimeter lining the castle. Such little space made it difficult for invaders to scale the wall.

Otto and Franco considered Kristoff a good, mindful guard who followed the correct hunches. And now he had a hunch something was wrong.

The clip-clopping returned and he watched the blackness, imagining where the sounds had originated.

Then he heard shuffling and faint clanks of a chain, followed by a soft thump. Kristoff grabbed the nearest torch from its iron holder and dropped it over the crenel. The little fireball whipped through the wind and hit the stone perimeter, but stayed alight, enough to illuminate what appeared to be a giant barrel propped against the castle wall.

Kristoff stepped back to unveil the cocked crossbow from underneath his cloak. He again loomed over the side to see fading torchlight suddenly flicker as an immense dark shape swooped by it. The clip-clops grew in speed and intensity. It was running.

Kristoff followed the sound, picking up his pace, not realizing he was running, tailing some unseen thing. Otto, from his position atop the wall walk spanning the gatehouse, saw Kristoff and abandoned his post to join him.

Kristoff noticed a deep grunting sound, made simultaneously with the clip-clops ceasing. He overran the point where the noises changed, unable to slow his momentum.

Two giant hands, their hairy brown fingers the size of sausages tipped with yellowed talons, latched on to a crenel ledge.

It jumped. No man can leap that high, Kristoff thought, unable to process the sight of talons boring through stone to tighten the grip of the thing dangling below.

He'd heard Otto speak of a hairy, cloven-hoofed, chain-wielding devil. Then the stories his parents had told him as a child came roaring back: how Saint Nicholas's dark other half pursued young deviants from one end of Europe to the other; how he'd swipe and stow them in his barrel to devour them alive in his cave, or tie them in an enormous weighted sack and toss them in the Rhine. The monster, the Krampus, would beat them into repentance with his ruten, and if he felt benevolent enough, allow them to live—Saint Nicholas gave Krampus considerable leeway, according to Kristoff's parents. No matter where the brats cowered, Krampus would find them.

Strained grunting, and then two twisted horns crested the crenel edge, followed by beady black eyes reflecting hatred in the torchlight. The beast opened its mouth and disgorged a red forked tongue, flicking it in and out to scare the guards who now lingered in disbelief around Kristoff.

One muscular tree trunk of an arm reached over the crenel to hasten the creature's crawl over the wall.

Kristoff's ears hadn't failed him all night—he'd been in enough battles to know the sound of a thrown knife splitting air, and the moment he saw a handle jutting from the thing's triceps, he braced himself for the roar.

The monster howled and lurched over the crenel.

More flitting—and two successive sounds of splitting skin.

Two throwing knives poked from its back, and for the first time Kristoff saw weakness and acted. He booted the monster in the face, sending it back over the ledge, but it still kept its grip and pulled itself up to glare at Kristoff, who fired a crossbow arrow into the monster's forehead. More roars. Then Otto, holding a torch, stood next to Kristoff.

"I'll die before you breach this castle." Otto jammed the torch into its face, sending aloft ember plumes. It released the crenel and roared the entire length of its fall.

Otto leaned over the edge and didn't see it, but heard a gloppy splashdown. He spit over the side. He stood and handed the dead torch to Kristoff, who remembered the sounds of chain links clinking, and seeing the barrel. He doubled back to the spot on the wall where he had earlier removed the torch to drop it over the side.

The fire hadn't died. Kristoff grabbed a second torch, aimed for the faint red spot, and released. The flames smacked down, and what Kristoff saw sickened him. He collapsed and sat against the wall. Otto ran to him and got on his knees.

"What was it? What'd you see?"

Kristoff, dazed, "The barrel's gone. It's alive."

Chapter Fourteen

Beate used the lingering roar to her advantage. She grabbed Heinrich's tankard, whirled, and crushed it into Wilhelm's face, knocking him over a table. Heinrich punched Mumfred in the diaphragm and then rammed his head onto a tabletop, leaving the steward in a dazed heap on the floor. Heinrich and Beate fled the great hall, frantic to find the inner courtyard.

Realizing they had not passed anyone as they ran, they slowed to walk out of the building, as if nothing had happened.

"We have to hide." Beate casually pointed toward the gatehouse. "We're trapped in here as long as the gate is down."

"Maybe not." Heinrich grabbed Beate's hand and they hastened their pace to the gatehouse, the interior of which was awash in candlelight. An oafish guard with a scraggly yellow beard wandered out.

"State your business."

"Lord Karl is allowing us to stay in the seamstress's and blacksmith's quarters for the evening, and that is where we wish to go," Heinrich said.

"Pleased to meet you. This is our first time in the castle. It's so…" Beate lingered for the word, "…majestic." She smiled at the guard. "And to sleep in one." She flirtatiously brushed her hand against his chain-mail-covered shoulder. "You are so lucky to do so every night!"

The guard sheepishly grinned. "Well, I mean, I get to sleep on the *floor*. I'm not a knight—not *yet*. I still must prove my worth to the baron and—"

"I am so sorry to interrupt, but Lords Karl and Wilhelm have provided us with so much excitement, I'm now woozy, and I really must lie down." Beate swept the back of her hand against her forehead.

Heinrich nervously glanced over his shoulder, looking at the great hall's moonlit entrance, dreading Mumfred and Wilhelm would burst from it.

"Well, all right. I remember seeing you two come in here with them. Enjoy your stay." The guard poked his head through the gatehouse door. "Open it!"

Beate and Heinrich bounced on the balls of their feet as the spiked door clanked open. "Thank you," they said simultaneously and rushed under it—Heinrich nearly scraping the top of his head on a rusty spike.

"She must really be tired," they heard the guard mutter, and then made their way toward the seamstress's quarters.

"We're not hiding in there," Beate said. "That's exactly where they'll look."

"Along with the blacksmith's," Heinrich said.

"Then *where*?"

Beate and Heinrich approached a cluster of six small apartments—one-room dwellings wedged together—lining the curtain wall. Two rooms appeared occupied based on the wavering candlelight visible through shuttered windows.

"Do we know any villagers who stay here who could hide us?" Beate said.

"Let's just knock and ask to come in." Heinrich approached the crude wooden door resting against the entrance.

"Anyone caught hiding us will be in as much trouble as we are," Beate said. "We can't endanger them."

She turned to Heinrich and her eyes widened. Heinrich pivoted, saw the danger and sprinted to save Beate, yanking her from the doorway where an arrow struck a second later.

"Stop them!"

They recognized Wilhelm's voice and saw, next to the raised portcullis, a dark figure pull an arrow from the quiver behind his back. They assumed the tall figure standing next to him to be Mumfred, and a third person, leaning against the wall in obvious distress, to be Karl.

Beate and Heinrich raced toward the stables built between

the curtain walls on the castle's left side. Arrows whistled by the couple and smacked the stone walls. Wilhelm ran alongside the gatehouse's front wall to intercept them. They charged by a corner and were momentarily out of Wilhelm's view. They knew he'd round the bend and see them taking shelter in the stables, which spanned the length between curtain walls, creating a barrier to the other side. It was their only option.

The two-tiered building had twelve stables visible from the front. Heinrich knew the leftmost part of the building, featuring a closed wooden door, housed the marshal. Someone was always inside, especially if guests were staying in the rooms built on the structure's second floor.

"Can you jump?" Heinrich called to Beate.

"I hope so!"

"Follow me!" Heinrich didn't slow as he approached the third closed stall from the right. He planted both hands on the five-foot-tall door, jumped and vaulted into the stall. Beate felt an extra kick of adrenaline and did likewise just as an arrow split through the stall door.

The unoccupied stall's rear opened up top so that a horse could loom over the rail. It was dark enough for the pair to hop that opening and stand in the aisle separating the twelve stalls visible from the front of the building from a dozen similar stalls opening behind the stables. A few horses poked their heads into the aisle, hoping for a carrot.

From their darkened position, Beate and Heinrich saw Wilhelm charging toward the stables along with more men—guards, they reasoned, summoned to hunt them.

"Do we cut through the stables and keep running?" Heinrich said.

"Uli!" Beate gasped, excited to see Heinrich's horse in the stall to the left of the one they had scaled. The horse eagerly dangled his head over the interior door so they could stroke him.

"I forgot that they housed him here after we arrived." Heinrich patted Uli from his forehead to nose.

Beate looked around. "I have an idea."

Chapter Fifteen

"What's good for the wretched, shit-smelling goose is good for the gander!" Perchta hid in the forest's shadows a distance away from the castle. She held a long knife at the ready as a foul monster—its barrel again strapped to its back—trudged toward her.

"If you'd be so kind as to return my knives," she said.

"First things first." The beast picked the crossbow arrow from its forehead as if it were no more than a splinter and snapped it in half with one hand and then turned its back to the hag. "Take them."

She lingered on her tiptoes to pluck the three throwing knives protruding from Krampus and then sheathed them in her boots.

Both stunk of fetid water and shit. The hag ripped the mucky fur cloak from her body and flung it into the woods. "I cannot fathom the cleaning bill on that one!" Her dress clung to her body and made wet sucking sounds when she moved.

"What about the rules?" Krampus said. "You went right for the castle's entrance. That was out of bounds. I was perfectly justified knocking you in."

"Are you serious? *Rules*?" Perchta tucked the long blade into her belt and wiped away the gunk that constantly trickled into her eyes. "I said that so you'd go around the side and give me a clear shot at the front."

Krampus shook himself like a dog, sending Perchta for cover behind a tree. She reemerged once the splatters against the trunk stopped.

He paid no attention to her and focused on the castle,

torchlight zooming back and forth along the wall walks. "They will be expecting me to jump again." Krampus turned to the hag. "Or are you expecting them to lower the drawbridge anytime soon?"

She eyed him, tapping her foot, and then glanced away. "No. I'm stumped about how to get in there."

Krampus again viewed the castle, looking at the outermost stone corner closest to him. "Hmmm. That might work."

"*What* might work?" She strode right next to him and repeatedly poked his ribs, demanding an answer. "Every guard and knight left in that castle will be lining the upper walls. If you so much as poke your big ugly mug between the battlements, they'll shoot or hack at it."

He didn't reply, but then his body flinched, not in fright, but in recognition of something so patently obvious that he was surprised it hadn't occurred to him earlier.

"Are we even here for the same person?" Krampus said.

"What do you mean?"

The giant reached into a small pouch that he'd nailed to his barrel and pulled out a tied-up scroll that mercifully hadn't been soaked with waste. He removed the twine and unrolled the parchment, looking for the desired spot. Finding it, he held open the scroll in both hands and shoved it in front of Perchta's face.

"There, the name that's not been scratched out—you see who I'm after?"

"It's pitch-black out!"

"What? Oh, yeah. I forgot. Hold this." He handed her the scroll. "Keep it open and wait right here."

Krampus lumbered toward the castle, emerging from the darkness and onto a patch of clear, flat rock under moonlight. The torches held by guards scrambling along the walls began converging in one spot, facing Krampus. He grumbled, out of annoyance, and then roared to announce his arrival.

From the castle: "Fire!"

Dozens of flaming arrows flew from atop the wall, arching like little comets to rain on Krampus, who hopped and wove out of the paths of all but one that sizzled straight toward his head. Figuring its trajectory, he stepped aside and, at the precise moment, tilted his skull sideways.

Perchta from within the shadows grimaced when the arrow struck. Then she straightened herself, realizing why he had deliberately made himself a target. Krampus trundled back and plucked the flaming arrow from the base of his left horn and held the burning stick toward the scroll in Perchta's hand.

"*Now* do you see who I'm after?"

She focused on the name that hadn't been cut through in red. She squinted at the slashes.

"Is that?"

"Yes, blood," he said, growing impatient. "Are we after the same person?"

"No. No, we're not." She handed the scroll back to Krampus and grew reflective, stroking her chin while watching the castle. "Then there was really no reason for us to fall into a lake of shit."

"We probably should have discussed all of this beforehand."

"I just assumed we wanted the same scummy urchin. I won't get in your way if you won't get in mine once we're inside," she said. "How do we get in there?"

Krampus slid off his barrel and plopped it in front of Perchta.

"What of it?" she said.

The monster pulled out a link of chain, bigger and heavier than the one he had used to slap her in the moat. The links kept coming.

"How can they all be in there?" she said.

He coiled the chain on the ground. "How did Jesus feed thousands of people with seven loaves of bread?"

She stayed quiet, and then said, "But why do you need so much?"

"To get into the castle."

"*How?*" she said.

Deeming he had enough chain, he pulled the last link from the barrel and left it in a pile. He then stomped his hoof on the ground, hitting dirt. He continued until he struck solid rock, and made a satisfied noise. "Get your knives ready."

Chapter Sixteen

Wilhelm, accompanied by two interior gatehouse guards—including the oaf, Bernd—and trailed by his ailing brother, entered the stables' small office and was greeted by Klaus, the marshal, who stood from behind a tiny desk.

Wilhelm, his longbow slung over his shoulder, explained the situation to the bewildered caretaker.

"I heard nothing, my lord. No sounds of disturbance. And nobody's been through here to access the second floor." Klaus motioned to a wooden stairwell in the back of the office, which led to the building's upper guestrooms.

"When was the last time you checked the stalls?"

"After the messenger and the two knights left to retrieve your father."

"Nice to know you've been sitting on your ass most of the evening."

Klaus, a former knight in his thirties who had assumed the marshal's job after a battlefield leg injury left him with a bad limp, blushed, then said, "I was about to feed the horses before you arrived."

"Then let's go feed them." Wilhelm, familiar with the layout, didn't wait for Klaus and passed through the office's small doorway that led to the stalls. Klaus hurried to light the four glass-covered lanterns hanging an equal distance from each other down the aisle.

Wilhelm's black courser, stabled in the stall immediately to his left, nuzzled the lord with his nose.

"Not now, Horst." Wilhelm leaned over Horst's stall door and saw empty space save for scattered hay and manure. "His water trough is dry, Klaus. Correct that."

"Aye, my lord. He'll get his oats too, as will your brother's horse."

"Karl's horse will likely grow obese this winter, as he probably won't be riding it until his penis heals."

"*What?*"

Karl stumbled in from the office. "For God's sake, Wilhelm, not everyone has to know."

Klaus, confused, turned to Karl. "My lord, is there something wrong with your horse's penis?"

"No, you moron!" Wilhelm scolded Klaus. "It's Karl's penis! Now feed the damn horses!"

Klaus scrambled for a sack of oats and avoided eye contact with Karl. Wilhelm took charge.

"Bernd, go to the second floor. Check the rooms just in case."

"Yes, my lord."

Wilhelm turned to the other guard, Anton. "You take the stalls to your left. Karl and I will check the ones on this side."

Anton nodded and got to work on the stall next to Wilhelm's horse. Karl took the opposite stall that was strewn with haystacks and a three-tined hayfork propped against the wall—an apparent makeshift storage area. He unsheathed a long dagger, slowly opened the swing door, and repeatedly stuck and slashed the hay. He rested after a few swings, his pain obvious. "No one's there."

Wilhelm observed and spoke to Klaus, who was pouring oats into the courser's food trough. "Is there hay like that in all the stalls?"

"No, my lord. Just the one your brother checked and the one farthest back on the left."

"Anton, I'll handle it," Wilhelm told the guard and then stalked to the stall in question. It too was piled with hay reaching his waist. Wilhelm drew his own knife, opened the door and kicked and slashed the straw. "Damn it."

He turned and saw in the opposite stall Uli's backside. Uli greeted the lord by raising its tail and defecating apple-sized blobs.

Wilhelm wrinkled his nose at the pungent smell and peeked

over the stall door: nothing but fresh shit and a few hay strands.

"He had a blade," Wilhelm blurted. Out of curiosity the lord extended his dagger and tapped the horse's saddlebags to see if the weapon might be stowed in one.

"I gave the porter the boy's knife, my lord." It was Mumfred, who had caught up to the hunting party and wore around his forehead a large white bandage, highlighted by a gooey red blotch in the middle. "They're not armed."

"As far as we can tell." Wilhelm watched Klaus pour oats into Karl's horse's trough. The brown animal was stabled two stalls down from Wilhelm's courser and eagerly began chomping its dinner. "No saddle." Wilhelm checked his courser, saw it wore no saddle, and examined two other stalled, unsaddled horses.

"Klaus, you unsaddle the horses, correct?"

"Always, my lord. We place them next to the stall doors for easy access."

Wilhelm confirmed this by scanning the ground, and then pointed to Heinrich's horse.

"Then why is this one wearing a saddle—"

Two bodies dropped from the beamed ceiling, landing on Uli—Heinrich square in the saddle, and Beate hugging him. "Go, Uli!" Heinrich slapped the horse's rear.

Uli nudged the unlatched exterior door, which crept open, and then slid out, building speed and galloping across the courtyard.

"Bastard!" Wilhelm frantically tugged his bow off his shoulder and in his clumsy haste swung it, knocking a lantern off its hook and into the stall behind him. He knew there'd be trouble when he heard the glass break.

Flames immediately clawed skyward as fire consumed hay.

"Move!" Klaus, holding a bucket, wobbled past the lord and threw water into the stall, but the fire spread too rapidly, triggering the horses to scream.

"Get out of here, everyone!" Klaus ran to first free the lords' stallions. Anton took care to release the other stabled horses. Bernd stuck his head into the stables.

"Nobody was upstairs—uh-oh."

Wilhelm stomped through Uli's open stall, and the fresh

manure, to freedom, and drew an arrow from his quiver. Two mares ran by him and he lowered his bow. He ran back into the stables, the fire licking the ceiling beams, to see Klaus had freed Karl's horse and was in the process of slapping the courser to run. "Wait!"

Wilhelm shouldered his bow, grabbed the saddle from the floor and said as he walked by Klaus, "Bring Horst away from stables. Now."

Wilhelm saddled and mounted Horst as the fire spread to the second floor. He looked through the flames to the other side of the stables, through which the couple had escaped, and breathed easier when he saw Karl and the others were safe.

He slapped Horst to run counterclockwise around the inner curtain wall. The horse thundered into the front courtyard, and for the first time Wilhelm noticed almost every castle guard had taken positions on the wall walks. He spotted Heinrich and Beate, still atop their horse, pleading with the front gatehouse guard to raise the portcullis and drop the bridge. Wilhelm grabbed his bow, drew and aimed at Beate's back, hoping the arrow would skewer her and Heinrich where they sat.

First came a massive boom. Then the bastion built to the left of the front gatehouse shook. The noise and vibration rattled Wilhelm. He fired and cursed because he knew he was off, the arrow whizzing by Heinrich, snapping against a stone wall.

A deafening crunch; more stones shaking; sentries posted within the battlements, frantic to get out; guards on both sides of the bastion firing arrows; some of the guards dropping where they stood.

Otto, from atop the wall walk, saw Wilhelm and screamed.

"Get to the bergfried! The castle's under siege!"

Chapter Seventeen

Otto looked from atop the wall walk to see flames rising within the stables. He could have sworn he saw Beate and Heinrich run and jump into the stables moments earlier.

"I hope that wasn't Lord Wilhelm who just ran in there." Franco, the burgmann, stood next to Otto near the castle corner to the gatehouse's left.

"Me too, but it's the creature that concerns me more." Otto, arms folded across his chest, ignored the mounting flames in favor of what hid in darkness beyond the bastion. The cloud cover suffocated any hope of moonlight.

"Whatever it is seems to be exerting a lot of energy." Franco, his longbow shouldered, a full quiver of arrows on his back, fitted a visorless barbute over his head.

Otto could only describe it as *crushing*—some brute force malleting earth. It happened every ten seconds: a determined yelp followed by an earthshaking pound. This repeated near twenty times until one of the thumps produced a quick crack. Then the pounding intensified, leading to what sounded like stone crumbling.

Guards, thirty of them by Otto's count, pressed against each other to view blackness through the crenels. Cold wind blew by the torches, whirling the flames, highlighting the men's grave faces.

A pained, straining roar startled the guards, and the lingering lament rose to what sounded like a satisfied "Ahhhhhhh!" followed by something incredibly heavy smacking the ground.

A few of the younger guards vomited over the wall.

That's when they heard chain links flapping and slinging

against—they couldn't say. But they knew whatever groaned and determinedly fiddled with the chains was preparing for battle.

"What about the baron's sons?" Franco asked Otto.

"What of them? They should be in their chambers, protected."

"Should we send someone to be with them?"

Otto surveyed the guards and noticed the chains had ceased clinking.

"I think we're going to need every last one of them here," Otto said.

Franco scanned the interior castle grounds. "You do realize the stables are on fire."

"Any other night, I'd be down there and so would you. The bigger threat's out there."

Franco returned to the unknown near the forest. "Could be a diversion, whatever's making the noise. The other sides of the castle are nowhere near as protected as this one."

Otto held his tongue, thinking it over.

"It's not an army—we'd have heard them massing. We have lookouts in the village who'd have charged up here if they knew someone was advancing. It's that thing."

The groan was quick, followed by the chain links clinking and something being rolled, thumping end over end, a distance away from the castle.

"Light it up!" Otto said.

"Archers ready!" Franco called. "Fire at will!"

The guards knew not where to shoot, so they estimated and fired at the spot generating noise. The arrows stuck dirt or stone and set nothing ablaze, but their fall gave flickering light to a massive figure twirling in place, clutching something.

"Keep firing!" Franco followed his own command and shoved an arrow into a torch. He shot the arrow, only to see it deflect off something it hit midair.

More arrows rained around the figure that steadily rotated toward the castle.

A few arrows struck the creature's back but didn't harm it. The dancing flames highlighted what they'd hit—a wooden barrel—and further revealed what was coming.

"That's it! I can see its horns!" Otto said. "But what's it hold—"

From Otto's vantage point, the monster briefly vanished, but the knight knew it impossible. The creature was still there, advancing as it whirled. Something huge momentarily blotted it out in a timed fashion.

The clouds parted, allowing the moon to bathe the ground in silver. The guards' eyes adjusted to see a monster circling clockwise, both fists entwined in chain. Tethered to the end links was a jagged boulder orbiting its master.

Franco saw clouds encroaching on the moon and knew time was short.

"Shoot it! Shoot it now!" He drew an arrow as he ran to the bastion's left side—the position allowing the clearest shot. He knew the two archers next to him as spectacular bowmen. "Aim for the neck."

No sooner had he said it when both guards crumpled facedown on the walk. Franco ducked below the crenel and pulled the nearest guard face up. The man's mouth appeared covered in mud, but Franco immediately recognized it as blood and saw it pulsing from the guard's neck around a throwing-knife handle. The other facedown guard's head rested in a slick blood pool of his own.

Franco couldn't conjure the words as two more guards, knives stuck in their throats, fell around him.

"Get out of the bastion!" It was Otto, yelling up to the guards fruitlessly firing arrows from the tower's windows.

Franco took cover behind a battlement and peeked down to see the monster's final rotation before the boulder crushed the bastion's base. The thunderous strike triggered stones to cascade into the moat. The beast roared and whipped back the boulder and in one fluid motion swung the rock to again pummel the bastion. The second impact shifted the bastion forward, the way a swift gut punch forces forward the breathless victim.

Otto too saw what would transpire with another direct hit. "Franco, get away from there!" The watchman stayed below the battlements and scurried from the shaky corner. Otto turned and surveyed the outer courtyard. The intense stable blaze combined with the momentarily bright moon lit the yard enough for him to see Lord Wilhelm firing an arrow. He knew not at what, but screamed for the baron's eldest son to get into hiding.

Chapter Eighteen

The boulder's third booming hit to the bastion's base sent spider cracks streaking up the tower, which began to shiver away its stones. The crumbling base could no longer support the tower's heavy topside. The remaining guards took their chances and jumped from the bastion windows as the tower groaned forward, toppling across the moat.

Beate and Heinrich ignored Wilhelm, for they knew everyone within eyesight was focused on the tower's fall. More inexplicable was the horned hulk that leaped atop the base's rubble.

A dagger tip pricked unsuspecting Heinrich's throat, and he and Beate, still mounted on Uli, looked to see Karl wielding the blade. A few feet away from the lord stood what they knew to be Karl's horse. *Karl rode here in his condition?* Beate thought. *He must really be angry at—*

"Get down or I kill him." Karl, one of his eyes twitching, edged the blade forward to draw blood. "You first, Beate. I insist."

"My lord." Beate's eyes glanced back and forth from the bizarre beast to the fledgling rapist. "Mad as you are at me right now, I think you should look at what's behind you."

"Get off the horse. Now!"

Heinrich felt the blade trembling against his throat. "Do it, Beate. We'll be all right."

Beate nimbly slid down Uli's side.

"Behind the horse." Karl motioned with his head.

She acquiesced.

"Beate, if you run, I slaughter Heinrich."

"She won't." Wilhelm, his bow shouldered, had caught up and, from atop Horst, snatched Beate's arm.

"Your turn, Heinrich," Karl said.

Heinrich slipped off Uli and stood next to Beate. Wilhelm had dismounted Horst and now clutched Beate from behind, holding his dagger to her throat.

"Wilhelm, should we kill them here or in the keep?" A star-rattling roar shook Karl enough to look at what every other soul in the castle was watching. The monster stalked down the stones, eyeing the hostage party the entire time.

"So, sticking something where you shouldn't!" it yelled toward Beate.

Her eyes widened. "Wait! You're mad at *me*?"

Both of the lords' horses took one look at the beast and shrieked as they ran from their masters.

Karl ignored the groin pain and slung himself atop Uli. "Wilhelm, come!"

The elder lord ditched the peasants and scrambled onto the horse. "Go!"

The lords rode Uli toward the second gatehouse, still open.

"Beate!" Heinrich dragged her into a run and they chased the lords.

"Are you insane?" she gasped, looking behind her as the thing glowered at them.

The remaining castle workers in the court swarmed the gatehouse like ants on sugar.

"I think we'll be safer in there than out here!" Heinrich said.

Karl and Wilhelm blew past the open gate. Beate and Heinrich saw Otto emerge with his broadsword from the pack of panicked people. He was joined by Franco and a dozen other chain-mail-armored, sword- and pike-wielding guards.

"Surround him!" Otto commanded the guards.

Krampus chortled. He still carried the thick chain and whipped it forward. Otto and Franco ducked as the boulder hurtled from the rubble and over their heads. Beate and Heinrich breached the interior gatehouse just as the rock wedged itself into the opening, preventing the portcullis from closing, leaving near the base a gap large enough for even the biggest knight to enter.

The monster dropped the chain and reached into its barrel for the ruten. Franco rose, his longbow ready, and fired. Krampus swatted the arrow with the switch and lurched toward the gatehouse.

"Attack!" Otto and the guards war-cried as they ran. The monster ducked and charged the two closest like a bull, skewering one on each horn, and stood so the twitching bodies could complete their bloody descent. It flicked its head, ridding itself of the corpses, and twirled with its outstretched ruten, smacking away swords and pikes, and crushing two guards in their faces. Otto barreled into the thing's chest, sending it on its back. Franco fired another arrow as the monster sat up, but the beast was too quick and seized the sizzling arrow before the tip could split its eye.

Two guards, their pikes pointed at the sitting creature's back, charged. Their battle helmets muffled a piercing shriek. The old lady arched over their heads, flipping in a circle midair, and landed in front of them. The guards continued charging, the beast's spine within sight, and as they passed the woman, they felt their stomachs burning.

They began stumbling and slowed enough for the monster to hear them. It stood, whirled and was about to strike with its ruten when the pair collapsed, a line of intestines trailing underneath them.

The woman flicked blood from her blades and walked into the fray. Six guards, Franco and Otto remained. The humans stood with their backs to the gatehouse, the inhuman walking toward them like they didn't exist.

"Don't cower! This is why you're here!" Otto yelled to his nervous guards. Arrows flew from atop the interior castle wall walks. Otto exhaled, buoyed by the sight of archers trying to take down the monsters.

Dozens of arrows poked from Krampus, who appeared a hairy, lumbering pin cushion—behind which Perchta hid for protection, but only momentarily. She sheathed her daggers and drew her remaining throwing knives and hopped to Krampus's side, aiming and releasing at lightning speed.

She smiled as three guards fell backward, causing the

remaining archers to cower behind the battlements.

"Stand and you die!" she screeched.

An archer ignored her and spun from a battlement to line up a shot. He hit the floor a second later, a throwing knife jutting from his left eye.

"See? I've got more!" she screamed, and then quietly to Krampus, "I'm out."

Krampus roared at the wall, keeping the scared men shaking where they stooped.

Franco stood next to Otto. Each of the men walked backward, in time with each of the monsters' forward steps.

"We'll be in greater numbers inside," Franco said.

The old woman slowly unsheathed her daggers from her back belt and grinned at Otto. Two guards standing to the knight's sides saw this and retreated to the gatehouse.

"I can't blame them." Franco's voice trembled. "That thing should be dead."

"I told that thing I'd die before I'd let it breach the castle," Otto said. "It's mine."

Krampus casually plucked the arrows from its body as it walked, and then reached into its barrel and pulled another stretch of chain, its links smaller in size, and brought it back like a whip. Perchta hopped behind Krampus.

Instinct told Franco and Otto to drop. Krampus swiped the chain sideways and ensnared the remaining guards in its links, bunching them together like bananas. Krampus jerked the chain backward and released it, sending the four screaming men over the bastion rubble and out of the castle.

"And then there were two," it snarled at Otto and Franco.

"Get into the bergfried with the lords," Otto said. Franco bolted but fell within a foot of the semi-obstructed gatehouse opening, a dagger through his back.

"After you," Krampus said, and with that Perchta bounded by Franco, retrieving her blade as she ran, and scuttled under the stone.

"Bravery. I appreciate that in my prey." The monster stopped ten feet from Otto. "But you're *not* my prey and no longer a child. So you now have the opportunity not afforded to your compatriots. Step aside and you live."

Otto held out his broadsword. "I pledged to the baron that I would protect his castle."

"And where is this baron of yours? Cowering in that big tower with his boys? I know a bit about the baron. He is a much better man than his children. But that is not saying much."

"Be that as it may." Otto stepped forward, his broadsword tip touching the monster's breastbone. "I pledged myself."

Krampus tsk-tsked. "A brave fool is still a fool."

Otto rammed the blade forward, but it snapped in half against this thing's stony chest. The knight, his mouth agape, looked at his broken blade. Krampus rammed the ruten against Otto's unarmored head, knocking the big knight sideways into the distant curtain wall.

Krampus scrunched under stone, mumbling, "I have a feeling my prey will not be as brave."

Chapter Nineteen

The boulder's impact to obstruct the gatehouse's portcullis sent Heinrich and Beate stumbling forward onto a frigid cobblestone walkway. They both looked up to see Mumfred, Wilhelm and three sword-wielding guards waiting for them.

"Karl's making his way up the churn tower now." Wilhelm pointed a dagger at the pair and then tilted it upward. "I trust there won't be any shenanigans while you accompany us?"

"Get up!" Mumfred kicked Heinrich's ribs, causing Beate to lean over her man and slap at the steward's feet.

"Such feistiness," Wilhelm said. "But I'd do as the good Mumfred says and get up. Or we can kill you both here. You decide. But I'm wagering my father would like to meet the peasants responsible for torching his stables, followed by a public execution to keep the rest of your filth in line." He nodded to the guards, two of whom rousted Heinrich to stand while the other yanked up Beate by her arm.

"Search Heinrich," Mumfred ordered the guards. The steward smiled at Beate and walked to her. "Perhaps there were some sharp things in that barn we should be aware of?" He cupped and massaged her breast. She closed her eyes and shivered. Mumfred drew his dagger and held it sideways, anticipating Heinrich's move. The blacksmith stopped, the blade tip tickling his throat. "Very good, boy. Now step back. And be searched like a man."

Two guards held Heinrich steady while the third patted him down. Mumfred inhaled Beate's scent while caressing her for weapons. "Nothing tucked in the waist, strapped to the thighs. Mmm. Delicious." The guards made Heinrich watch while

Mumfred's tongue lingered up Beate's neck.

"He's unarmed," said the guard who had searched Heinrich.

"As is his woman," Mumfred said.

"Come, Beate," Wilhelm said. "I'll be sure to wash you in preparation for Lord Karl. My brother might not be prepared for intercourse, but I'm thinking he's eager to fuck with you all the same."

Two guards tumbled backward over the wall walk, one landing on cobblestone, the other flat on Beate. She screamed as arterial blood gushed onto her face and chest, such was the knife wound to the guard's throat. She frantically pushed the guard off of her and sprang up, shrieking and wiping blood from her eyes.

"We'll definitely have to bathe her now." Wilhelm chuckled and then, realizing the severity of the situation, said, "Let's go."

The guards pushed the pair to walk behind Wilhelm. Mumfred, dagger still drawn, prodded the chagrined lovebirds through a sea of panic. Castle workers rushed for whatever protection they could find within the great hall and its surrounding rooms. Guards, their swords, axes and pikes ready, stood behind the boulder, waiting for—they hoped—the knights to slip through with welcome news of smitten enemies.

The party walked through the great hall and exited through the building's rear to see, by its lonesome, the bergfried. Beate, her face still smeared in red, gawked at occasionally lighted windows leading to the churn tower—the spired top surrounded by four bartizans.

A dozen guards swarmed the group and then backed off when they realized Wilhelm was leading it.

"Lord Karl's up there, escorted by two men," one of the guards said, and yelled to those behind him. "Bring the steps!"

Beate looked for the entrance but couldn't find it. Then, upon seeing a tall wooden stairwell built on a rolling platform, it dawned on her that the entrance was deliberately designed to be inaccessible. The guards aligned the steps with a closed door built thirty feet above ground.

"Open it!" Mumfred called to the guard peeking through the iron-barred, circular window framed next to the door, constructed from two wooden planks fastened as one by iron studs and crisscrossed with iron bars—making it harder for enemies to chop down. The door opened and the guards finished pushing the stairs to the entrance. Wilhelm ascended first, followed by a guard, then Beate and Heinrich, who were prodded by the remaining two guards, with Mumfred bringing up the rear.

Beate entered a gloomily lit stone stairwell that wound clockwise upward. She didn't see Mumfred, but heard him call to the exterior guards, "Destroy the stairwell."

"How will we get out?" Beate didn't realize she'd blurted it until Wilhelm poked his head from behind the guard in front of her.

"My dear, the only way you're leaving this tower is by being thrown from it. Whether it's from thirty feet up and possibly surviving, or one hundred feet up and assuredly dying is up to you."

Dimly glowing lanterns hung from wall hooks. Beate and Heinrich breathed stale and dirty air as they climbed. They occasionally passed small rooms with closed doors. Beate remembered, prior to entering, seeing windows in the tower and figured guards—likely armed with bows and arrows—had sequestered themselves within to watch the action.

She yearned for a sword to slice off Wilhelm's head and mimed swinging a blade with her right hand, which smacked against the spiraling stone interior.

Clever, she thought. *Unless the attackers are all left-handed, fighting while climbing the stairs won't be easy.* She then envisioned Wilhelm, gripping a sword, turning toward her and slicing downward—his right hand relatively unobstructed by the outer wall.

What else have they thought of? Thick walls? Fortified rooms? That thing destroyed an entire curtain wall, so I don't think it'll be discouraged by a locked door.

The stairwell wound into a closed door. Wilhelm pounded on it.

"It's us! Open it!"

A wooden slat at eye level slid sideways and revealed a

squinting guard illuminated by lantern flame. He nodded and closed the peephole.

Beate heard people laboring opposite the door, moving heavy things, setting them to the floor. The door swung open and revealed an octagonal room with closed doors on every wall. Four guards greeted the party and then hurried them inside.

"That thing's on the move," a crossbow-toting defender said to Wilhelm. "It made its way through the second gatehouse and killed whoever was down there."

Wilhelm gulped. Beate saw him sweating under the glow of numerous lanterns.

"We've not seen it approach the bergfried—if that's any consolation," the guard said.

Beate grinned when she saw how tightly the guard gripped his crossbow, to the point where the weapon shook. Then she recalled the monster chiding her for sticking something where it didn't belong. *Karl deserved worse*, she thought. *I can't believe it's angry at me for doing that—unless it has a penis and imagined what it must've felt like to have a needle jammed…*

She turned pensive and held Heinrich's hand.

"Karl?" Wilhelm said.

The guard glanced above to a closed ceiling door built into the stone, twelve feet from the floor.

"Took a little bit for him to get up there, but he's all right."

Wilhelm glanced over his shoulder. "Let's get cozy."

The guards moved everyone to clear the stairwell entrance and closed the door. Two guards grabbed a thick metal plank and placed it into horizontal iron grooves at the entrance's base. They repeated the process with two more beams—one placed at the door's midsection, the other up top—to practically conceal the door, making it near impossible for someone to ram through.

"Karl!" Wilhelm looked at the ceiling. "I know you can hear us. It's safe."

The younger lord fumbled with metal, and then Beate heard him strain while lifting the small, square door inward. A wooden ladder slid from the darkened interior and thudded to the floor. Two of the guards that accompanied Wilhelm's party scaled the ladder first.

"After you, Heinrich." Wilhelm extended his arm. "Try anything when you get up there and my men will kill you on the spot.

Heinrich looked at Beate, who nodded, indicating *It'll be all right.*

He climbed the rungs and Beate went to follow, but Wilhelm held her back. "Not just yet." Wilhelm looked at the guard with the crossbow. "How are we on water?"

"We have enough buckets for a few days if it comes to that. I'm assuming the baron will return with a small army to get us out of here if that thing's not defeated first."

"Find some rags, as clean as possible, and use them one by one to wash this young woman." Wilhelm grabbed a lantern hanging from a wall and held it to Beate's face. The guard grimaced.

"It's not her blood," Wilhelm said.

"I'll take care of it, my lord." Mumfred appeared before Beate, holding a long white bandage, which he proceeded to cut into squares with his dagger.

"I had some extra on me just in case my head started to bleed again." Mumfred scowled at Beate. "I'll take the chance that it won't."

"Just don't taint the drinking water," Wilhelm said. "Send her up when you're done." The lord climbed up and left Beate surrounded by Mumfred and the guards. One opened the door opposite the one to the stairwell and returned with a carafe of water.

"Yes, this will do." Mumfred smiled as he dipped in the first square and then brought the cold water to Beate's chest, washing her neck but deliberately sliding his fingers under her bloody garments to fondle her nipples.

"Just pretend that I'm Heinrich and it'll go quicker." Mumfred finished with her face by the fourth square and stepped back to admire her. "Not pristine, but nice enough to be kissed, I think." He looked up the ladder, seeing nobody looking down. "Perhaps I'll try first."

Mumfred seized her shoulders and advanced, but halted when a roar—a noise he now knew well—wound its way up the stairwell and pummeled the iron-slatted door. The guards in the room turned to the entrance, and for several minutes all was quiet. But soon frantic footfalls ascended from behind the door, followed by fists pounding against it, and numerous male voices. "Open it! For God's sake, open it!"

Chapter Twenty

Anyone brave enough to heft a weapon surrounded the bergfried, a square tower that touched no other building or wall. Ladders—if they were tall enough to reach an opening—could be propped against it from the ground. But the lower windows were no wider than a man's face, and no ladders were long enough to be leaned from a wall walk and settled against one of the bergfried's upper sections.

The tower's designers had cut machicolations into each of the four bartizans' overhanging floors, allowing for guards to see the bergfried's base, and the ability shoot arrows down at enemies or pour boiling, putrid liquid onto them.

"The windows near the ground are too small for us to sneak into—especially *you.*" Perchta elbowed the monster while eyeing the bergfried from a crenel built atop the solar's roof. Anyone who was really looking could see Krampus's two horns poking from behind the battlement next to her. The great hall and its adjoining rooms reached halfway up the bergfried's base. No man could run and leap from the hall's roof to grab any part of the bergfried without falling and dying. She edged her eyes over the crenel just enough to see scores of guards, five deep, wreathing the base.

Krampus peeked above the battlement. "But not the windows higher up."

Perchta looked. "True. Big enough for a man to lean out and fire at the masses. But do you honestly think you can jump up there?"

He mulled it, assessing the hall roof's length. "Not enough space for a running jump." He rose to watch the guards circling the tower below and spotted the bergfried's elevated entrance. "It would be easier for me to jump through *that* doorway after you climb down the tower's stairs to open it—after I throw you through one of those upper windows." He pointed to an illuminated window framing a guard resting his elbows on the stone edge.

"That's a possibility." She nodded and then furrowed her brow. "Wait, *what*?"

He practically wrapped his entire hand around her waist and yanked her backward, her feet dangling above the roof.

"*Don't* scream," Krampus said. "We can surprise them."

He didn't wait for a reply but threw her like a javelin toward a window built three-quarters of the way up the tower.

Krampus figured any guard worth his salt at some point might expect to see Perchta—just not the crown of her skull appearing out of nowhere and smashing his face.

The guard fell backward as Perchta speared through the open frame.

The room's firelight shimmered violently and then resumed its calm waver.

Perchta's silhouette filled the frame. She held a dagger out the window and pointed to the entrance below. Krampus never took his eyes off it and began knee-bending, preparing to jump down, waiting for the right moment.

The guards immediately in front of the entrance didn't think anything amiss when they heard the door clank to unlock.

"Coming out!" Simon, a pike-wielding guard directly under the entrance, called. "Be ready!"

The man next to him leaned in. "We broke the stairs, remember?"

"We've got the ladder. Don't worry. Chances are they want to lower buckets for water."

The heavy door creaked open. No lantern light. No noble or guard popping out to demand or request. Only darkness.

"My lord? Wilhelm? Mumfred? Who goes there?" Simon smiled when Marco, the guard who regularly manned the entrance, appeared in the frame. Enough men below held torches to illuminate Marco's face.

"Marco! What's the matter?" Simon tilted his head all the way up. "You look—" Warm water splashed into his eyes, and he grunted as he wiped it away with his free hand. *Only water isn't supposed to be dark.* Simon looked at his fingers and then up to see Marco a moment before impact.

Simon crumpled to the ground, Marco's midsection covering his face. Simon released his pike and spastically waved his arms for help. Two guards lifted Marco and gagged as his entrails spooled around Simon's face. The horrified guards dropped the body, allowing the corpse to resplatter Simon, who at that point took matters into his own hands and pushed Marco off of him.

He screamed as he jumped to stand, frantically wiping offal out of his eyes. Everyone watched the beleaguered guard and almost at the same moment realized that whoever killed Marco likely was hovering thirty feet above them.

They jerked their heads up in unison to see the butt of what appeared to be a hulking mountain goat using its hooves to propel itself up the wall and scurry into the entrance.

A long log-thick arm tipped with talons darted out, grabbed the door's interior handle and yanked it shut. The sound of the door locking lingered around the bergfried's base.

Simon, panting, cleared away enough gunk to see what was going on and then spoke calmly to the nearest guard but loud enough for everyone to hear.

"Go get the ladder. We'll likely need it. And I suggest we spread out—away from the base."

Nobody argued, but one faceless guard in the back spoke up: "Why?"

Simon retrieved his pike and began walking away while looking at the churn tower high above. "I fully expect it to begin raining bodies."

Chapter Twenty-One

Beate climbed into the lords' protected perch. Wilhelm pushed her to the ground the moment she arrived, pointing a blade at her.

"Be a good girl and behave."

Two guards scurried down the ladder and drew their swords. Wilhelm, after withdrawing the ladder, lowered and locked the door. Beate didn't know how many men occupied the bartizans as lookouts, but figured every guard, and Mumfred, stood before the stairwell entrance, scared to open it.

The octagonal loft, as Beate came to think of it, stood as tall as the room below it, although with windows on four walls and lanterns hanging from all eight. Save for a few sparse furnishings and a table holding a few more lanterns, there were blankets and pillows on the floor. She eyed a large water bucket and a couple of cabinets—likely stuffed with rations, she reasoned—against two of the walls. She spotted the ladder next to the closed floor door.

Still on all fours, Beate glanced at Wilhelm. "I suppose if we're meant to cower, we should do it in comfort."

He smiled and withdrew the blade. "Indeed. I've been up here a few times when the castle was under attack—unsuccessfully, as you can imagine. Nobody's ever managed to scale the entrance below."

"Until today." She took her time grinning.

Wilhelm, unamused, "Stand."

She rose and for the first time saw Heinrich slouched against the wall directly behind Wilhelm. Her beau's hands were bound behind his back, his ankles roped.

Karl sat on a three-legged stool next to him and feasted on Heinrich's discomfort. "Are you ready for the show?"

The blacksmith glowered at the younger lord and shook, trying to free his hands.

"I know how to tie a rope, trust me." Karl stood. "Wilhelm, please sit next to Heinrich to make sure he doesn't get frisky."

Wilhelm sheathed his dagger and plopped next to Heinrich. Beate saw Wilhelm's bow and quiver propped by the older lord's side. A sheathed sword and dagger rested before the longbow.

"This can go a couple of ways, Beate." Karl spoke calmly, as if addressing a child. "You can be a good girl, not resist, and perhaps live long enough be executed before the baron."

"The second option?" Beate backed herself against a wall as Karl crept forward.

"I torture you with a knife, slowly. People in the village will hear your screams."

"The third option?"

"I said this could go a *couple* of ways."

Beate pressed her sweaty fingers against the frigid wall. "Then I suppose the former."

"I thought so. Take off your clothes."

Beate stared at him, not answering, until, "I will not. I don't see how that would do you much good, what with your lame penis."

Karl stopped five feet in front of her and balled his fists. "Maybe I will keep you alive long enough until I heal. And do to you what I intended to do earlier. While your man watches. I'll spare him the sight of things now and let him think about what I'm doing to you." He turned to Wilhelm. "I'll be all right. Take him below to the cell."

"Very well. It's your twisted revenge, not mine." Wilhelm unsheathed his dagger and pointed it at Heinrich. "Up."

"The cell?" Beate said.

"One of the many doors you saw down there upon entering," Karl said. "One leads to a stone room with a barred window. A precaution just in case we find a traitor in our midst and need a place to put him."

Wilhelm unlocked and lifted the floor door and directed

Heinrich, who hopped to the edge of the opening. "You first."

"How can you expect him to climb down a ladder with his hands and feet tied?" Beate said.

Wilhelm replied by pushing him through the floor's hole.

"Heinrich!" Beate lunged for the opening, but Karl backhanded her.

"Stay back!"

Wilhelm peered over the hole. "Don't worry. He's moving." He called down to the guards, "Get him out of the way!" He waited a few moments and lowered the ladder. Just before his head disappeared, he spoke to Karl: "You can handle this?" He glanced at the ladder.

"Leave it open, just in case you need to get up here in a pinch."

Wilhelm vanished.

Karl backed away from Beate, his eyes never leaving her, and opened one of the cabinets. Beate felt sick when she saw him holding rope. She put her hands behind her back.

"Very good, Beate. I don't want you to worry, because what I'm planning to do won't hurt you physically—that much. You already observed that my, well, *body* doesn't work the way I'd like it to. But my tongue does."

He advanced, preparing for her to dive for the floor's opening. "If Beate climbs down, kill her!"

She bit her lip.

"I thought as much," he said. "And those guards will be up here the second I call them." He held up the rope. "Understand?"

Beate nodded. "I will not come to you. Whatever you do to me, you'll have to come get me." And there she stood.

"That's it? *That's* how you're protesting?" He walked toward her, still on his guard. "I expected better, given everything you've put me through today."

Her jaw fell. "What *I've* put *you* through? You can go to hell."

"I've paved my way there in brimstone. Now, turn around and show me your hands."

"I'm not doing a damned thing for you. You want me to turn around. Then you make me do it."

"If you say so." Karl shrugged his shoulders and grabbed for her arm. Beate brought both hands forward and joined them, thrusting up and into Karl's midsection. He gasped, dropped the rope and grasped a knife handle. Beate punched him in the nose. Karl stumbled backward and fell on his butt.

Beate screamed toward the floor, "Karl, no! Not that! Please don't!"

She heard chuckling and knew Wilhelm's voice. "My brother can be such an animal."

She focused on the breathless lord and continued her faux protestations. "I wanted to wait for my wedding night before doing anything like that!" She kicked the side of his head and he was out. Again toward the opening: "That's not natural! The tongue was never meant to do that!"

More guffaws.

She gripped the blade, realizing that Karl's fit midsection and layers of muscle had likely saved his life. She'd plunged only halfway the throwing knife that she'd swiped from the dead archer who had fallen onto her from the second gatehouse. *Thank goodness Mumfred had just searched me and didn't think to do it again*, she thought.

Her mind ran through scenarios: *I climb downstairs, I'm dead. Wilhelm or the guards could climb up here, I'm still dead.*

"No, Karl! Please don't shut the door! It's bad enough what you're doing to me when they can listen!" She yanked up the ladder and kicked closed the door, which muffled even more loathsome laughter.

Then it hit her. She ran and opened the cabinet. Thin, coiled rope sat on a shelf.

I just hope there's enough.

She slipped out the rope and assembled a mental game plan, unaware that Karl had regained consciousness and crept behind her.

Chapter Twenty-Two

Perchta trailed Krampus up the stairwell as he swiped away guards with his ruten. When they came upon a closed door, Krampus yanked it off its hinges and Perchta dove in to slaughter whoever kept watch within.

Guards heard the commotion and descended the stairwell to find a nearly ten-foot-tall horned monster beating guards with a birch switch, and a gruesome, haggard lady disemboweling whoever was behind him.

The men fled upstairs. If they encountered a closed door, they warned the guard inside to join them. "You're dead if you stay in there!"

A dozen guards had reached the top steps and the frontmost men pounded the door, pleading for refuge.

More than halfway up the tower, Krampus found a locked door, tucked his ruten under his arm and pulled the handle with both hands. Stones gave way, and he flicked the door down the stairs as Perchta scurried inside.

A surprised guard dropped his crossbow at the sight of a double-fisted, knife-wielding crone. He climbed onto the window's ledge and judged how far he'd fall. Then he looked up, and Perchta saw fleeting happiness in his expression as he jumped and plummeted, screaming until Perchta heard the distant life-ending thump.

She leaned over the ledge to see the pancaked guard and then glanced above the window as Krampus scrunched through the doorway. "What's the holdup?"

"I know why he jumped," she said, eyeing the heavens. "Keep the guards busy. And be ready."

Chapter Twenty-Three

Any trace of laughter on Wilhelm's and Mumfred's faces vanished as the guards' pleas from behind the churn tower's closed door grew more desperate.

"It's coming! I can hear it!" called one voice.

"Open it! Please! Have mercy, my lord! There's still time! We'll be quick!"

Wilhelm and Mumfred, daggers drawn, stood behind the phalanx of guards.

"My lord, it *would* allow for more protection in here," Mumfred said.

"Why chance it? Opening that door even for a moment would give those things the advantage. Those men are supposedly among the bravest in the castle. Today they can prove it."

The door shimmied and rattled on its hinges, and the men's caterwauling devolved into gibbering laments.

The roar silenced all.

Blades cascaded to the ground, clanking and sliding down the stairs.

"So much for proving their bravery," Wilhelm mumbled, and then called to the guards before him, "Fight to the death, men!"

They twisted their heads, looking cockeyed at Wilhelm.

"I will not abandon you," he said. "If you fall here—so shall I."

The ceiling door drew upward. Wilhelm and Mumfred stood directly below and moved aside just as the ladder hit stone.

"Wilhelm, Mumfred, come up now," Karl called. "You must see what's become of Beate."

Wilhelm, knife still in hand, scurried up the ladder without eyeing the guards—many of whom grunted to convey *Thought so.*

"I'm not much good with a weapon and would get in your way," Mumfred said while climbing.

Wilhelm waved for Mumfred to hurry and then ripped the ladder into the room and secured the ceiling door.

Wilhelm breathed easier and turned to his brother standing near the cabinets. Beate waited by his side.

The older lord assessed the girl. "So what's become of her? I don't see much difference."

"Drop your dagger," Karl said. "You too, Mumfred."

"What's wrong, my lord?" Mumfred said.

"I'd do as he says, Mummy." Beate slid away from Karl, and into view came a little old lady holding Karl by his neck scruff, a dagger tip to the base of his skull.

"Do it, Wilhelm," Karl said.

Wilhelm and Mumfred released their daggers simultaneously.

"Kick them this way, please." Perchta tilted her head toward the cache of weapons in the corner and the pair obeyed. Beate grabbed Mumfred's dagger.

"Move away from Mummy, Wilhelm." Beate ambled toward the steward and placed the blade tip to the warm flesh below Mumfred's Adam's apple.

He gulped, the pulse moving the blade.

"Open the door, Mummy. Make a sound and Karl dies."

The grinning hag pushed the knife into Karl's neck, drawing both blood and whimpers.

Beate stepped back and Mumfred dutifully lifted the door and lowered the ladder.

"I'd like you to go down first, Mummy."

The steward steadied himself with one foot on the floor and the other on the top wooden rung, which provided a perfect archway for Beate, who kicked to break stone.

Mumfred shrieked, lost balance and fell through the hole. Wilhelm rushed to the edge. Beate, watching him, cautiously glanced through the opening. Mumfred's back faced the ceiling—as did his face. His neck had twisted, the skin shaped like intertwined rope. His eyes remained open. Guards circled the body and looked up.

"I'm not going to kick you, Wilhelm," Beate said. "You're to climb down and command the guards to disarm and to open the door. Those are *her* orders." Beate waved her dagger to Perchta. "Not mine. So I wouldn't disobey them."

"Let's go, Karl. Baby steps." Perchta pushed the young lord to limp forward. Wilhelm descended and stood at the ladder's base. Karl stood sandwiched between Beate and Perchta.

"Like we discussed, dear." The hag removed the blade from Karl's neck, and Beate's dagger took its place. Perchta dropped through the hole and seized Wilhelm before she landed. She held her blade across his throat so all the guards could see.

Wilhelm closed his eyes and slowly raised his hands to reassure them.

"Open the door," he said.

"My lord?" A couple of guards spoke in unison.

Wilhelm hissed through gritted teeth as the hag slowly dragged the blade—not to cut, but to raise every hair on his body.

"Men, lower your weapons and open the door."

Karl labored down the ladder and was trailed by Beate. She eventually stood behind Karl and tickled the back of his neck with her dagger.

"Open the door and no harm shall come to you," Perchta said.

Still, the guards hesitated. One ventured, "What about the thing behind the door?"

The door boomed once and rattled.

"Open this door and your fate will be that of the men around me," came the monster's voice.

"But you killed them all!" said the guard closest to the iron slats.

"No, he didn't," said a terrified guard from behind the door. And after a few moments, "But I fear he could easily change his mind."

Two of the guards within manned up and dropped their

weapons and removed the top slat. Another pair did likewise to the middle section. Soon the door was clear. One of the guards unlocked it and tugged, and the door flew open as an avalanche of frightened guards spilled in and scrambled across the room to make way.

Hooves clopped on stone and the beast emerged, pounding the ruten in its palm. Perchta took over.

"I take it my furry friend is being more benevolent than I care to see," she said. "Drop your weapons—not that they've been doing you much good anyway—and leave the tower and the castle. If I see even *one* of your faces when I get down, I'll gut you and make your loved ones watch. And the same goes for anyone who's currently defending the bottom. They already know I'm serious based on what I did to the man at the door."

Every guard turned to Krampus, who emphatically nodded yes. One by one the men dropped their weapons and walked single file out of the room and down the staircase. Krampus extended his ruten to stop the line, leaving three guards in the room.

"Take *that* with you." The beast pointed to Mumfred.

Unquestioning, the men grabbed arms and legs and made off with the corpse.

"Heinrich, where's Heinrich?" Beate pecked the blade into Karl's neck, pinpricking it with blood.

"That one." He pointed to a door smaller than the main entrance, similarly barred with iron slats, which prevented escape all the same.

"Get your hands dirty for once." She pushed him hard. Karl glared at her, affronted, and straightened himself with whatever dignity he could muster before hobbling. He labored to dislodge the beams, and once successful, he unlocked the door.

"Step back!" Beate said. And Karl did. "Heinrich, come out! It's safe!"

The blacksmith warily nudged the door and glanced from behind it. Seeing the weirdest assemblage of characters he'd encountered up to that point in his life, he eased himself out of his small cell. His arms and legs still bound by rope, he hopped across the room to join Beate, but first stopped before Karl and viciously head-butted him to the floor. Once Heinrich was reunited with Beate, she cut the ropes to free him.

Karl mewled while pushing himself up, and fell against a wall for support.

"Poor baby." Perchta withdrew the blade from Wilhelm's neck and left him standing alone, powerless.

"How the hell did you get up here?" Wilhelm grew more nervous with each step she took toward Karl.

She pointed her curved blade at Beate while passing her. "The girl secured a rope around the cabinets and tossed it from the tower's window. Apparently it took her a few tries to clear the bartizan."

Beate nodded, feeling victorious.

"You were going to climb down?" Wilhelm said. "Nonsense."

"I'm deathly afraid of heights," Beate said. "So no, rappelling down a tower was out of the question. But I had a feeling she'd find her way up if she saw the rope. And she arrived just in time to save me from your wretched brother."

Perchta stood behind Karl. He pressed his cheek against the stone wall and closed his eyes to avoid her. She stood on her tiptoes and whispered into his ear.

"The only thing worse than a rapist"—she licked his earlobe—"is a child rapist."

Karl repeatedly blinked, absorbing the accusation, and glared at her. "I've done no such thing."

"Is that so?" She scratched his cheek with the blade. "Lying won't help your situation."

"I'm not!"

She backed away, allowing him to confront her. He looked at her and to the blade and back.

"Yes, I rape women. But I don't touch children."

"I know!" she cackled, unable to suppress her laughter. "I was just having some fun with you."

With that she screeched and pounced on Wilhelm, driving the blade through his chain mail and into his diaphragm. She landed on him and shrieked while crudely dragging the knife toward his waist. Wilhelm's wordless screams turned to gurgles as she repeatedly grabbed and plopped intestines into a slippery pile next to him.

Content with her work, she stood and began scouring the room. "Curses! I lost my sack in the moat. Maybe I can improvise." She turned to Karl. "Do you have any straw up here?"

Karl, both hands covering his mouth, his eyes bugging at Wilhelm's dying body, turned to Perchta and shook his head.

"I thought not." She tucked her dagger into her belt and spotted a carafe of water about a quarter full on the floor. "My hands are a fright. If you'll excuse me."

Realizing she still held a dagger, Beate marched Karl back against the wall, the blade to his throat.

"How many women—*girls*—have you raped?"

Karl's eyes focused on the knife stinging his neck. "Many. Too many to count. But only girls of marrying age!"

"Like that makes it acceptable?" Beate spat in his face. "Why? Why do you do it? You see what it causes!"

"Because I can." His sinister tone chilled Beate, who backed off. "I'm the baron's son." He straightened himself. "To reject me is to invite death. And there are so many to choose from in the castle. The knights usually have pretty wives, and that makes for luscious daughters." He licked his lips. "Some of the knights even know it but say nothing because my father will butcher them if they do anything to me."

She gasped. "Your father *knows* about you?"

"Ideology and family always trump conscience. Call it an insurance policy. Sure, my father's disappointed when I tell him which noble's daughter I've most recently conquered. But he's got enough money to pay off whoever complains the loudest. Had you not shown up, that lumbering idiot Otto's daughter would've been on my menu. She's about the right age. Believe me—I wish you'd stayed in that shitty village of yours. Speaking of which, Wilhelm stuck with your ratty peasant children because who'd take their word over his?"

"I can't be bought," Beate said.

"I bet your parents can."

Perchta wiped her hands dry on her dress and joined Beate.

"As for you, Karl." She drew both daggers.

"Good." It was Heinrich. "Too many innocent people have died today—Gisela, her baby. This worm actually deserves what's coming to him."

"He's right." Beate blocked the hag's path with her arm to stay her. "What you did to Gisela was inhuman. *Why* did you kill my friend? She was innocent!"

"Trust me, she was not."

"That she suffered the way he did"—Beate eyed Wilhelm—"I cannot imagine she deserved it. But you—" She looked at Karl and then hesitated, stroked away a tear and spoke to Heinrich. "How did you know Gisela was pregnant?"

Heinrich shrugged. "I heard it around the village."

"No." Beate slowly circled Heinrich. "No, you didn't. Gisela said I was the only one who knew. Me and the father."

"Uh-oh," Perchta said mischievously.

Krampus lifted Heinrich by his shirt and held him an arm's length away. "You've been naughty."

Beate approached Krampus. "Sticking something where it doesn't belong—you weren't talking to me. Heinrich was right next to me. My God. Gisela was fitting you for our wedding too. And you were away with your father in early December when—" she waited for Krampus to look at her, and when it did—"when you were hurting people."

The monster flashed its eyebrows.

Heinrich, dangling like a marionette, clutched Krampus's arm so he wouldn't fall. "Beate, listen. Gisela came on to me and—"

"Oh, don't even try that!" she said.

"He's right." Krampus shook Heinrich. "But your boyfriend here did nothing to stop her."

Everything swarmed around Beate, enough for her to massage her temples. To Perchta, she said, "So, you're not here for Heinrich?"

"Heinrich is Krampus's concern." Perchta pointed a dagger at Wilhelm. "I came for that pompous perversion on the floor."

Beate looked at Wilhelm's pale corpse and back to Perchta. "You equate a premarital affair with child molestation?"

"Gisela—your dearest friend—knew full well you were to be wed and violated your trust in the worst possible way by becoming *his* whore." She disgustedly gestured at Heinrich. "Had *he* put the moves on Gisela, *he'd* be the one with a belly full of straw."

Krampus brought Heinrich close enough to kiss him. "Lucky you."

Perchta sidled up to Karl, whose bravado vanished.

"I might not have come for Heinrich, but I did indeed come for your brother."

"And not me," Karl said.

"I specifically said 'I came for that pompous perversion on the floor'. I didn't say I came *only* for him." Perchta's blade slid over the ragged belly wound Beate inflicted on Karl.

He shook uncontrollably. "Please don't!"

"I was going to carve off your penis first, then your balls, and *then* gut you. You'd be praying for a needle through the cock by that point."

Karl blubbered. "I promise I won't do it anymore! You can come for me if I do! I know you'll be able to find me! Please! Spare me!"

"Very well, I will." She stowed her blades and walked to leave the churn tower.

"What?" Karl and Beate said it together.

"I'll admit it's tempting to finish you off now. But recent events have convinced me to spare you for a little while."

Karl looked at Krampus. *"Him?"*

"No. I came here for Heinrich and Heinrich alone. But I agree with the frau. I have a hunch you won't rape anyone ever again."

"It's time for you leave, Karl." Perchta gestured to him and waved her hand forward. "After you!"

Karl took two steps toward the doorway. "You're not going to kill me from behind?"

"I give you my word, for what that's worth," she cackled.

"And you only came here for Heinrich?"

"I already said that, Karl," Krampus said. "How the master missed you is beyond me, but sometimes names slip through the cracks. I would've had *fun* with you."

Karl then turned to Beate, who still held a knife. She answered before he spoke: "I've harmed you enough already, Karl." She dropped the blade. "Your survival is in your hands."

The younger lord smirked. "I can pretty much survive anything—if this day is any indication."

Karl turned to exit and was met by Otto standing in the doorway. At first Karl thought himself rescued and then recalled what he'd said earlier.

He raised his hands for calm. "Otto, how long were you out there?"

"Long enough to say the day's not over yet, my lord."

The broadsword-wielding knight, despite being cut, battered and bruised, nimbly moved and punched Karl in the gut, leaving him on the floor, breathless.

"Go, all of you."

Perchta had already left. Beate tapped Krampus's leg to get his attention. "Don't kill him, please."

"Thank you, Beate! I knew you'd forgive me!" Heinrich looked at Krampus's scowl, and then to his bride-to-be, who sported a similar visage.

"I asked him not to kill you, Heinrich," she said. "I didn't say he couldn't *punish* you."

Krampus chuckled and carried a whimpering Heinrich down the darkened stairwell.

Beate turned to Otto. "Now what do I do?"

The knight kicked Karl's face, laying him flat, and then pinned him with a heavy boot. "Stay here tonight. Go back to the village in the morning. Others will too. Travel in a group. I will come to check on you, although it may not be for several days. The baron *will* return, and he won't like what he finds here. But you're in no danger from anyone in the castle. I promise you that."

"Thank you."

Otto recalled the first time he'd seen Beate that morning, indifferent to the girl's plight, but no longer. "I know Gisela hurt you, but nothing justifies what happened to her. And Heinrich's piggish betrayal doesn't warrant murder either."

She thought about it. "I don't think the Krampus will kill him. I hope he doesn't."

Otto applied pressure to keep Karl still. "You're young, Beate. You'll find a deserving man." He glared at the young lord, who appeared on the verge of hyperventilating. "So will my daughter." Then to Beate, "Take time to grieve, wait for things to return to normal. A good life is still possible, despite all of this."

She laughed to herself, an inexplicable cackle. "Normal? I relied on a lunatic harpy—my best friend's murderer—to save my life tonight. I gave a giant monster permission to beat up the man I had planned on marrying next week. I view everything that Heinrich, Gisela, Wilhelm and Karl did as immoral. But to those monsters—the Krampus and Perchta—all of that twisted behavior *is* normal. It's why they exist. I woke up this morning happy, blissfully unaware that everything around me was fraudulent. My *normal* life was a perception void of skepticism. Surviving Twelfth Night taught me I can't let that happen again, if I'm ever to trust anyone." She smiled at the knight. "Thank you for your kindness. I don't mean to be dismissive."

"I didn't take it that way. You should be on your way, though. Take care of yourself. *That*, I know you can do."

"I appreciate that."

She took her first step down the stairwell.

"Beate, wait." Otto said. "You can do one more thing."

She turned. "Yes?"

"You can say goodbye to Karl."

Chapter Twenty-Four

A few days later

The three of them spread a large piece of parchment across a flat stone that served as a table within a torchlit cave rarely seen by human eyes.

When one finished scouring the immaculately penned document, the reader gave a small, greasy candle to the next participant in line. And the process repeated itself twice more, leaving the contract checkered with wax droplets.

"Is everything in order?" the old man said.

"Yes, master."

"Frau Perchta, are the terms to your liking?"

"Bavaria's mine except on December fifth, and on occasion December sixth, and if your hairy underling can't finish the job on either of those days, he waits until next year and doesn't rear his ugly head until the next December fifth. No exceptions. Is that what I'm reading?"

"Correct, and what will you do?" the old man said.

"If whichever miscreant your goon was after manages to elude him on December fifth or sixth, he'll let me know who— and if that same miscreant is on *my* list, I leave the wretch for Krampus to catch the next December."

"Splendid."

"And what if I cannot get one of *my* marks in January, and I provide you the name and that kid is on Krampus's list the following December?" she said. "Does Krampus leave that brat for me?"

The old man pointed at the contract. "Go to section B, subsection D—third paragraph."

"Oh, for goodness sakes!" Perchta pored over the document, mumbling words as she read them, and then out loud: "It is left to the sole discretion of Saint Nicholas whether Krampus may pursue one of Perchta's failed attempts from the previous season, seeing that Perchta has twelve days to mete out punishment or reward, and Krampus only has, at most, two days." She smirked, tapping her foot, ruminating over the terms. "Wait, why is it up to *you*?"

"The child who eluded you could redeem himself or herself the following year, and in such a case, the child might be on my list for reward. And I imagine if that is the case, you would consider slipping the child a coin. Am I right?"

"Well, that *rarely* ever happens," she said. "Once bad, usually always bad."

"There are exceptions," the monster said.

"Nobody asked you!" She threw up her hands. "Okay, fine. Where do I sign?"

Krampus pushed her out of the way, pricked the pad of its forefinger with its thumbnail and scratched its name in blood across one of three blank lines.

"I *have* a pen." The old man held up a quill feather.

"I've got work to do." The monster pointed to a gagged, roped young man quivering in the cave's corner.

Perchta grinned. "I'll take the pen, thank you." She watched Heinrich shake as she wrote her name.

The old man scribbled last and then rolled up the parchment and tucked it under his red robe. "Now then, do you need an escort out, Frau Perchta?"

"I can find my own way." She fiendishly smiled at Heinrich and turned to Krampus. "Can I watch?"

The monster, not looking at her, slipped its ruten from the barrel on its back. "This is between me and him. And I will not begin until you leave."

The old man gripped a long crosier and held out his hand. "Come, Frau Perchta, I shall accompany you."

She grunted. "*Fine.* Maybe on the way out you can explain to me how you came across that big lummox. Was it like finding an abandoned puppy?"

The old man chuckled. "Not exactly, and I prefer to keep some things secret. Otherwise every saint would want one."

She shook her head and walked beside the old man through a dark tunnel.

"Perchta." The monster's voice reverberated around the walls.

She ducked back into the cave. "Yes?"

"I like you."

"Well, isn't *that* sweet?" She waited for it to reply, but Krampus stayed focused on Heinrich, who'd closed his eyes and seemed to be praying. "Thank you. I suppose. And I agree with Beate. Do not kill him."

Krampus looked at her. "Do you think it is okay if I eat some of him?"

Heinrich's eyes bugged out and darted back and forth from the monster to Perchta, who tilted her head, expressing *Really?*.

Unseen by Heinrich, Krampus gave her a quick wink.

"Oh, well if *that's* the case, his legs look scrumptious." She cackled and left to catch up with the saint.

About the Author

Matt Manochio lives in New Jersey with his son. He worked as a newspaper reporter for 12 years, and the highlight of his journalistic career was meeting AC/DC and interviewing vocalist Brian Johnson for USA Today.

Other Books by Matt Manochio

The Highwayman
Sentinels
The Dark Servant

Curious about other Crossroad Press books?
Stop by our site:
http://store.crossroadpress.com
We offer quality writing
in digital, audio, and print formats.

Enter the code FIRSTBOOK
to get 20% off your first order from our store!
Stop by today!